Circle of Grace

Olwyn Harris

Reading Stones Publishing

Stock image provided by Shutterstock: www.shutterstock.com
Cover models are AI generated images courtesy of Canva.com

Published by: Reading Stones Publishing
Helen Brown, and Wendy Wood

Cover Design: Wendiilou Designs
          Wendy Wood

For more copies contact the publisher at:
Glenburnie Homestead
212 Glenburnie Road
ROB ROY NSW 2360
Mobile: 0422 577 663

Email: Readingstonespublishing@gmail.com

Dedication

For Sue, who for years prayed with me through all sorts of times…

Fallowhytes

1882

Then Hannah prayed and said:
"My heart rejoices in the LORD;
The LORD makes alive… and raises up.
He lifts the needy from the ash heap;
He seats them with princes and
has them inherit a throne of honour.
It is not by strength that one prevails…"
(1 Samuel 2:1, 10)

1.

"Your name is Hannah, Miss?"

"You sound surprised... or shocked. Why would it be shocking that my name is Hannah?"

"Well..." He looked at her amused. "You are a lady. Hannah is a name for housemaids and cooks."

"Really? 'Housemaids and cooks'?"

"I know dozens of houses that have a Hannah on staff. It is common knowledge that the first criteria of having Help is that you must have at least one Hannah at your disposal. Preferably two."

"Actually, my namesake was a woman in Scripture who was gracious and strong in the face of great harassment and loss. Her outstanding legacy had nothing to do with whether or not she was a lady. I am not embarrassed by such a name... even if it is not glamorous."

"Perhaps that is what I find curious. You strike me as a lady who has great potential for *glamorous*."

"I hardly find that flattering. I would hope that my demeanour is more sensible and sincere than glamorous. You are not doing yourself any favours, Mr Digby, with your attempts to sweet-talk me."

"Well, to my credit – I did say potential." He grinned again, charmed by her frankness and unwillingness to be complimented. "Your card is not getting much attention tonight. Would you like to dance?"

She shrugged. "Perhaps. But I am here with Lady Whitmore, so I will first go and see if she needs anything."

That confession alone had been sufficient to discourage a number of potential partners.

"Whitmore… of Whytehaven Hall? She is the paragon of English aristocracy."

"Yes. She is."

"You have done well to secure her as your patroness. But do you really think that old Biddy will want to dance with you? I feel slighted that your preference is for her company," he said with a quizzical frown.

"Mr Digby! Your reputation for rudeness precedes you! Whether you feel slighted or not is of no concern of mine. Please excuse me," she said with the fall of frost in her voice.

He reached out and touched her arm. "Promise me, when you are released from your obligation to amuse her that you will have at least one dance with me," he insisted.

She stopped and stared in surprise. The warmth of his hand felt strange against the chill of her manner. "Really, Mr Digby, I am not at all amusing enough for your taste."

"You are wrong, Miss Hannah, because I find you extremely entertaining. One dance?"

"There are plenty of other dancers here tonight who would be willing partners."

"Oh, but none quite so beautiful as you."

She nodded and acknowledged his refusal to be put off. "Very well. If I return here before they start the next set, then you may have the quadrille." She had not the slightest intention of accommodating him.

"I am here-forthwith planted to this spot. Go… fulfil your obligations so you may return."

Hannah shook her head and left. Lady Whitmore sat on a sofa supported by cushions. "Hannah my dear, have you acquired at least one dance on your card?" She turned over the card on Hannah's wrist as she reached across to adjust a cushion. "Nothing? Not one? This was the condition of us coming."

"We came so that you could enjoy the music and the spectacle of the fashion and dances. And it is quite the spectacle."

"Yes, yes. I know what we agreed. But it goes both ways dear. You will never improve yourself without proper attention to details. Acquaintances and associations are such details."

"I did not come here, Lady Whitmore, to attach myself to a beau. I am content enough in my station."

"Pish-posh and twaddle young lady! There is always room to improve. You don't have to betroth yourself… just have a dance. You like dancing. Go on… as we agreed. Or I will insist on inviting that rather obnoxious young man with the loud voice, large sideburns, and large fortune to dinner. Regularly."

"M'Lady, whom you invite to dinner is entirely your prerogative."

"But it will not only be me who will have to suffer. Go, do as I ask, and save us both the vexation of such company."

Hannah sighed. These people were not her people. In truth she was more entertained as if watching through a window from out on the street. Why would Lady Whitmore insist she join their world?

After intermission, she returned to where she had left Mr Digby. She had hoped he had become bored or thirsty or was lured away by company more to his taste. But he was standing there, mildly telling a story that had his audience in laughter. He spotted her and his eyes jumped. He quickly concluded his tale and excused himself. "I am delighted that you have reconsidered and consented to entirely perfecting my evening."

She rolled her eyes and didn't even try to mask her distaste. "Really Mr Digby, I am here under the threat of another less agreeable obligation. Lady Whitmore was quite uncompromising in her insistence."

"The discerning Lady Whitmore can see that I will be good for you." He bowed slightly with a grin on his lips and a twinkle in his eye.

Hannah frowned. "She has no idea who potentially would be my dance-partner. So do not feel flattered that your company is for my betterment."

"Regardless of whether the celebrated Lady Whitmore is informed of your good fortune to dance with me, it does no harm to have some fun and to enjoy oneself while the sun shines."

"It is after dusk, and I believe the proverb is intended to value industry and productive service: making hay while the opportunity of sunshine presents itself – and it has nothing to do with frivolity or the amusement of a dancehall."

He tilted his head, and his amused grin was broader. "Ah... but you are here and not in the fields with the corn-stooks. So then, let us call it a harvest rollick and take advantage of the opportunity while we can. They are forming the quads." He held out his hand and with a lively hop in his step joined the closest set of dancers. With extravagant enthusiasm he danced and laughed and jollied Hannah through the steps. She did enjoy dancing and it was not many turns before she added a smile. She spun with a laugh and stumbled on the last turn. Digby caught her and drew her back from the formation, as the other dancers concluded the dance with a flourish and clapped their partners. The music paused, and she realised he still held her, so she quickly stood up tall; regaining her composure, she smoothed her skirts.

He gallantly bowed. "Now that I have saved you from the gross humiliation of being trampled on the dance floor, you are indebted to me for preserving your life. I am unquestionably owed another dance," he said as he took her arm and guided her to the drink counter and offered her a glass. "So, which dance on your card will be my payment? You have to concede that you are in my debt."

"No, Mr Digby – the only concession I will allow is that I'll introduce you to Lady Whitmore."

"Why would I want to be introduced to her?"

"She asked for it. As evidence that I have been engaging in a dance."

"Well, that sounds entirely to your benefit, not mine. I have no reason to be introduced to her."

"Mr Digby! Your arrogance knows no bounds. She is one of the most genteel, generous, and accommodating people I know."

He smirked again. "I tell you what. Pay your debt of gratitude – for saving your life – with a dance. Then, if you would have me comply with your demands of introduction so you can save face with the formidable Lady Whitmore, you will need to concede to yet another dance."

Hannah closed her eyes and took a breath. "That price seems entirely too high, but I am not in a bartering mood, so let us get this over with. And then, yes, come and meet Lady Whitmore."

The ensemble struck up the introduction for a country polka, so he extended his arm and escorted her to the floor. They were both proficient dancers and easily assumed command of the floor. With ease he took the lead and Hannah matched him step for step. The music concluded and she quickly curtsied and escaped to the fringes of the dance hall to catch her breath. He followed her there and grinned as he extended his hand when the music resumed almost without pause, settling into the demure tempo of a genteel waltz. "Come, your debt is paid. Have this dance with me. I am decided. I really do require an introduction to Lady Whitmore," he coaxed.

She sighed and he led her to the floor again.

"Always the flatterer, Miss Hannah. Three dances! How could one resist such urgency to be in my company?"

"Sarcasm is not befitting one of your standing, Mr Digby."

"Well, it seems you are a hard one to please. Jokes and wit do not please. Cynicism is treated with equal scorn. Is this a case of refusing to dance with the flute or weep with the dirge?"

"It seems I have not refused to dance, and the only lament here is over your appalling manners and frivolous conduct."

"I have only endeavoured to be engaging and civil. You, on the other hand, have endeavoured to be disengaging and aloof." His grin became broader. "And yet I have prevailed because here you are dancing with me: thrice. Do you think the whole room is watching us?" And he spun her around with a flourish. The music cadenced and they paused.

As she curtsied, she glanced around. Indeed, it did seem many eyes were on them. "Come, let me introduce you to Lady Whitmore," she said quickly.

His blue eyes glinted, and he nodded, duly walking with her over towards the chairs set out in social arrangements to the side. "My Lady? As you requested, may I introduce you to my dance partner for this evening: Mr Sebastian Digby. Mr Digby, this is Lady Bridget Whitmore."

He bowed gallantly and murmured his greeting. Lady Whitmore glanced up at him and tilted her head to the side. "Did he behave himself, Hannah?"

"He is an accomplished dancer. There were no missteps on his part."

"You won't mention my chivalrous rescue during the quadrille?"

"No need – that particular debt was paid by dancing the polka. That is all the mileage you will get out of that, Mr Digby."

"And then the waltz…"

Lady Whitmore raised her painted brow. "Three dances? Well now, you must be exhausted. Hannah dear – please fetch us all a fresh drink. You. Sit here."

Hannah blinked as he compliantly sat beside her with a mischievous grin. The man was completely impervious to normal manners. Everything was a joke for him. She turned and went for the drinks as instructed.

Digby watched her leave with a chuckle as Lady Whitmore turned to him. "Well, this is a pretty state of affairs. You are completely besotted. But this is not the first time a handsome girl has taken your fancy."

"Come Aunt Biddy, you didn't tell me you were acquainted with such elegance. You were holding out on me."

"Sebastian, you are not going philandering with Hannah. She is not your type."

"Oh, but she is! In every way she is. Already she has told me I am rude, arrogant, and sarcastic. She is fearless, and I am absolutely smitten."

"None of which is to your credit young man."

"But, Aunt Biddy... ever since I can remember, you have been on a mission to improve me. You have relentlessly told me to better myself over the years. Here is a very good reason to do just that. You should be pleased."

"And just how are you going to accomplish that? You are the third son of an indebted earl who has no recourse since his fortune is almost entirely spent. You are not going to get a penny, and your only inheritance is an obscure title."

"Well, the upside is that I didn't inherit his bad temper and I won't inherit his debts. Besides I have you."

"Me? Good grief, Sebastian, I wiped my hands of you long ago."

"Oh no you didn't. You regarded my mother too well. She told me on her deathbed to disregard your huffing and puffing because, even as her cousin, you were closer family than my own brothers."

"You diminish your mother's memory with your reckless behaviour. I will not have her maligned so."

"I have never lived outside my means… and you know it. Besides, what others do not know… or what they assume, keeps them out of my pockets. There can be no disappointing expectations when people expect so little."

Hannah returned with the drinks and carefully handed them over.

Sebastian took his with a nod and raised his glass as he turned to Lady Whitmore with a glowing smile. "Well thank you, Lady Whitmore. It would be my pleasure to accept." He stood up and offered Hannah the seat he had been occupying. "I have been invited to the Hall to sojourn during the hunting season. It's been a while, and I think it is entirely time to revisit some of these time-honoured traditions."

"Whytehaven Hall does not conduct hunts," said Hannah quickly. "They haven't for many years. M'Lady you seriously can't have invited him?"

Lady Whitmore smiled and shrugged. "Life has been entirely dull for far too long. It won't hurt us to be amused for a time. More congenial at least, than the company of Lord Sideburns."

2.

Sebastian stepped down from the carriage with a confident tread. The footman dropped his trunk firmly on the drive and reloaded the step before the horses rolled on. He entered the drawing room as Jeremy, the steward, announced with a bewildered tone: "Mr Sebastian Digby?" He shrugged and then added under his breath, "He insisted, M'Lady. Lord knows why."

"Lady Whitmore! Thank you again for your kind invitation. This will be entirely too much fun!"

Hannah stood in the corner looking at some books and turned as he entered. She shook her head. Would he determine whether an invitation was commendable based on its degree of 'fun'? She couldn't believe his superficiality. Could someone really make a lifestyle out of being ignorantly perky?

He turned to her and bowed. "Miss Hannah. It is a pleasure to see you again."

She nodded curtly and closed her book sharply. There was no pleasure on her part. He noted that with a smirk and chatted over a cup of tea with Lady Whitmore before he retired to settle into a guest room.

Hannah knocked at his door to deliver strict instructions that Sunday dinner was a proper occasion regardless of the number of guests, and he was required to present himself dressed accordingly. "I don't want Lady Whitmore to be embarrassed," she concluded.

He grinned at her formal manner. "I am delighted on two accounts. Your concern for Lady Whitmore's comfort, and by the prospect of a 'proper' Whytehaven Hall dining experience," he observed with a chuckle. "Your determination to educate me will surely be enlightening." Hannah frowned, nodded, and left him standing in the corridor.

Lady Whitmore entered the dining room on Hannah's arm. She was dressed for company with a fair smattering of ruffles, while Hannah wore a simple gown and attentively saw to Lady Whitmore's needs as she was seated at the head of the table. Lady Whitmore was barely settled when she stood up again. "Jeremy! Rearrange the table settings so we can all converse without having to use a hearing trumpet. How can we enjoy good conversation so far apart? Yes. Yes. Right up here with me. Let us take full advantage of this little occasion."

"Yes M'Lady." Jeremy shuffled the settings as requested.

Sebastian looked like he would burst into rollicking laughter at any moment. Eventually he was seated on Lady Whitmore's right, Hannah on her left. The soup was served.

Hannah was very attentive to Lady Whitmore and made no effort to respond to Mr Digby or his attempts to engage in conversation. But he told a good story and as they ate their way through their second course, even she was reeled into his various tales of woe or adventure that had Lady Whitmore chuckling with amusement. To see her so entertained was compensation enough for enduring his company.

"So, Hannah my dear, did you realise that Sebastian…"

And he knocked his wine, and it spilt out over the table. He quickly dabbed at it with his serviette, shuffling the crockery, mumbling his apologies in a completely unrepentant manner. Hannah looked annoyed and Lady Whitmore sighed patiently. "Hannah dear, will you do Mr Digby the courtesy of fetching another wine from the cellar?"

"The cellar, M'Lady?"

"Yes. I fear Jeremy has not served the best wine if Mr Digby has resorted to spilling his drinks. Choose another bottle."

Hannah shook her head confused but duly complied. As she left, Lady Whitmore turned to Sebastian with a raised brow. "Well?"

"Aunt Biddy! You can't tell her of our connection. She doesn't realise."

"I know she doesn't realise. That was why I was going to mention it."

"But it is so much more fun for her to think I take liberties."

"You *do* take liberties."

"Yes, but the liberties I take are based on family connection and long-standing affection... not audacity and pluck. I'd like her to think I am *plucky*."

"Plucky? Sebastian you really have a very peculiar sense of a good time. You must truly be bored with this life you have. When will you consider some real occupation?"

"Bah. That sounds entirely too dull. I would much rather tell some good stories... and watch her gasp as I presume to be familiar with her esteemed patroness."

"Hmm. Well, I'll leave this particular story for you to tell, but on the condition that you do it before you leave. It is only fair she knows the lay of the land. I insist."

"Oh, Aunt Biddy… even for you… that sounds so very grim and responsible."

3.

They walked about the garden, and on Sebastian's cajoling, they swapped story for story, on any topic he introduced. Hannah was shocked that after she had shared a particularly heartfelt experience that he only offered a wry smile in return. "I hardly see how that is amusing, Mr Digby. You have absolutely no sense of proper decorum."

He shrugged. "I am just wondering which tale is the more pathetically tragic. Your parents, who loved and indulged you with every opportunity and had the audacity to die. Or mine… who were spiteful and a trial… and have had the audacity to remain alive."

"Mr Digby!"

"It really does seem completely beyond the realms of respectable. How dare they die… or live… as the case may be. We are hereby thrown into each other's company because of their inconsideration."

Hannah closed her eyes and frowned. Could it be possible he actually held a level of insight that insisted on masquerading as insincere? "We have no obligation to be dictated to by the circumstances that are presented to us, only to do well in spite of them."

"Miss Hannah, that is entirely too sensible. I have allowed myself a whole lot of license for the insensible over the years, because of my pathetic and deplorable upbringing. Yet you will not give me even a yard of string."

Hannah shook her head. "Mr Digby, you are responsible for your own choices and direction."

He huffed and shrugged. "Bah! Why? It is convenient for me to have an excuse. This has been my mainstay defence my entire life. Would you rob me of this very credible justification of mediocrity?"

"Mr Digby, I am being serious. You cannot be in jest over something so grave."

"See, Miss Hannah. You are serious enough for both of us. I have no need to get in that sombre line, because I think it has been worn out by utterly too much traffic. My line… the queue of optimism, is in fact far too neglected by society in general, and you in particular."

"That is because I don't believe life is a joke. It is outrageous how you insist on being so blithe."

"Your protest is that I have too much good-humour? Really, Miss Hannah, you show me I am not the only one with capacity for the absurd!"

"No, that is not what I meant. But I insist there must be a place for the serious and the introspective. Yet you ignore those moments entirely."

"Ahh… but do I?"

"Of course, you do. You never offer a solemn reflection on anything!"

"Never? Well, I confess I hesitate to allow you to witness such clear-headedness. But does that mean it doesn't happen… ever?"

"But why would you hide such a thing? This is something which I admire greatly."

"Ah-hah! So, you feel cheated that I do not give you grounds for such admiration? You want to like me. I am encouraged!"

"But I cannot appreciate a blank slate. There is no content to admire. I esteem the qualities of sincerity and thoughtfulness."

"Hmm. Thoughtfulness. What would you like me to think thoughtfully about? Throw me a line, Miss Hannah, and I will reflect thoughtfully away."

"Oh? Umm… well, all right then. What do you think about the insistence on traditions such as the foxhunts?"

"Really? The topic on which you choose to plumb my contemplations is sports? Now you do make me laugh, Miss Hannah!"

She turned away indignant. "In some circles the hunts are becoming controversial. You seem like a man who enjoys his sport. I thought you may have an opinion on it."

"Well, I am amused to think this is a topic you consider worthy of your time. I thought with such an open invitation you might have gone for the gullet on temperance, or social welfare, or the women's suffrage movement. Instead, you default to entertainment. Humph! And I assumed you would scorn such superficial customs. You surprise me, Miss Hannah."

"I didn't say I approved. I attempted a topic on which I thought you were familiar."

"Your accommodation of my limited and meaningless experience is touching. Yet to be entirely honest, I have no right to voice an opinion on this particular topic, as I have never participated in a hunt."

"Really? Never? But you told Lady Whitmore that you wanted to revive your experience of the tradition and hence your invitation here to Whytehaven Hall."

"Traditions I generally do not mind, but I find to use the natural habits of harmless creatures for such brutal theatre entirely repugnant."

She raised her brow. "You are harsh on your social class, Mr Digby."

"See, I can hold an opinion. Not that anyone cares to hear it. Generally, it is more amusing to keep it to myself, and go fishing for other people's dogma. People can be quite zealous about the most insignificant matters."

"Like what such matters?"

"Like… silk versus cotton. Plain versus plaid. Pinched versus pleated. Dun versus chestnut. The colour of my horse is entirely immaterial in my mind… yet I sat at a card table once where the performance of the team was judged entirely on the colour of their fetlocks. Who knew that this fundamentally serious matter could be so earnestly debated at such length? I timed them for three hours before even my tenacity for the ridiculous reached its limit. And still the controversy was never resolved. I have no idea whether white, black, or dun is better."

Hannah smiled. "You enjoy drawing attention to the nonsensical."

He shrugged. "You have to admit it offers entertainment that requires no effort to conjure up."

"And the conservation of effort deems it worthy?"

"Yes, it would seem. It leaves energy for more serious matters… like fox hunting."

4.

"Today is the day, Miss Hannah," Mr Digby announced as Hannah walked through the door.

She looked up. "It is?" She had delivered Lady Whitmore her tray and came to the kitchen for her own cup of tea. She preferred to keep breakfast simple.

Mr Digby had evidently hollowed out a place for himself in Willis' territory, sitting comfortably at her deep panelled bench. Willis didn't seem disturbed that this gent was contentedly presiding in her culinary kingdom, cup in hand and toasted bread on the plate in front of him. In fact, she looked very pleased to have this tall, good-looking man eating her food in such an unconventional setting. That was unexpected: Willis was usually quite territorial, and a stickler for etiquette when it came to visitors.

"It is, Miss Hannah. Today we go on a lion hunt!"

"Oh really, Mr Digby? Whytehaven in Autumn is hardly the setting for a Safari. The season is cool, and our grounds are not large. And no lions at all, as far as I know."

"Such a quest is not restricted by acreage or climate... but by the spirit in the adventurer. I cannot allow that this type of excursion is only relegated to the domain of the African colonies. Since you find fox-hunts repugnant, we will have our own English Safari. You will accompany me."

"Will I now? I am quite sure I am required here."

"Not at all. I have covered it off with Lady Whitmore and she releases you at ten o'clock. Although she expects a full report on our return. Do you own a riding habit?"

"I do." Even Hannah conceded privately to herself, that to get outside for the morning could not be entirely irksome. "But I will not shoot, and I will not fetch."

"Then I will have to do my own shooting and fetching. The exercise will do me good."

Hannah shook her head and went to fill her cup. Willis grinned and Digby laughed. Then he spoke to Willis in earnest tones about some safari inspired deliciousness that would be suitable for a picnic.

Hannah went over to the stables at ten, and as she walked in, Digby was laughing with Jeremy and the stable-hand. She noted their private jokes, and wondered if she would always be excluded? She expected that from elite social sets, but the servants also held her apart. She wondered where she fitted. Not there, not here. Yet she noticed, with a little confusion, that it seemed Mr Digby traversed all territories and engaged with all manner of folks with equal ease... and wherever he went, people welcomed him with open arms. He was probably right. An African safari would be as comfortable as the socialite dancefloor for him. Both would be adventures to his carefree spirit. In some ways she was tempted by his unencumbered frivolous disposition. In other ways she found it uncomfortable, common, and improper.

He bowed and handed her a cylinder on a strap. "Your weaponry, Ma'dam."

"I told you I will not shoot."

"Ahh... and I promised to fetch. Just take it. No lives will be lost this morning by this arsenal."

"You make no sense, Mr Digby."

"And you make no fun. Come. Even dressed for riding, you look elegant. Please note the white fetlocks on both our mounts. I feel the evidence is increasingly being weighted in the favour of white."

She smiled and despaired of ever having a sensible conversation with him.

"Jeremy has been telling me of all the good haunts, so I think our mission will be entirely fruitful," he said enthusiastically.

"You should know… I am not an experienced rider."

"No matter. Leisurely is the requisite of what we do this morning."

As he hoisted her up into the side-saddle and he realised her appraisal of 'inexperienced' probably more accurately meant she had barely sat on a horse at all. She refused to admit fear, and he noticed with a raised brow how she clung grimly to the saddle horn until her knuckles knotted with tension underneath her gloves. He ambled their horses from the stables and turned out over the low bridge along the waterway towards the fields and forested grounds. He stopped and dismounted in a clearing and quickly came around to help her down. Hannah wobbled ungainly and took a moment to steady herself on his arm. When she had found her land-legs, she cleared her throat, stood up and looked around. They were in a small clearing where an obscured bird-hide held the view out over a small lake.

"Bring your cylinder," he said. He took the strap from his shoulder and extracted a small maritime telescope. "You see, hunts don't have to include slaughtering the innocents.

It can be just as amusing to have a leisurely ride around the estate to find all the foxes' lairs and bird-hides."

She stared at the card he pressed into her hand, with a bemused furrow on her brow. "A hunt with no shooting?"

"It does however require a deadly, steady line of sight. It's true: the rules of *'Feathered or Furred'* are quite established. You have to write down as many live creatures as you can capture in your sights. This card has one column for feathered, the other for furred. The one with the most unique entries at the end of the day wins. The victor gets to dictate whatever activity they want of the other person; but it must be within the week."

"I have never played this before. Not even heard of it."

"Oh, it is not a game to be trifled with, Miss Hannah. It is quite serious."

"Serious?" She laughed and shook her head. "You've just made it up!"

"Oh, it is indeed serious. The stakes are high. I will get to extract an activity of my choice out of your company. See. All your coaching to take things seriously has paid off. I am in your debt."

"Which means you now owe me."

"Touché. Let us double the stakes then. An activity to the winner of each category… one for the Feathered column and one for the Furred… both to be conducted within the week."

"You only say that because you think you have already won. But do not underestimate me, Mr Digby. I can hold my own."

"Hmm. We will see. Lady Whitmore has promised to adjudicate any controversy, and I have bought a book in case we need to reference any unknown specimens."

"Oh, a heron!" she cried, and they went to work scribbling and scanning and jotting.

After a while he looked at his pocket watch. "That's half an hour. Next place. Follow me." They ambled the horses to the next stop in a wooded belt of trees where the leaves were turning golden yellow in the crispness of the autumn air. A large, fallen oak served as a haven for all sorts of animal and bird life. After the allotted half hour, they rode onto a rise overlooking the amber coloured forest that ran down into a meadow. Then again, they moved on and stopped the horses on a grassed bank covered in a blanket of leaves with a brook running along a moss-covered rocky border. "This will be our Safari Lunch stopover. There is even dining for the horses," he said as they dropped their heads to eat. See we don't need lions on a safari to have a wonderful time."

"This is a diverting version of a fox hunt. But we haven't seen a fox. I think it is the wrong time of day. Early morning would prove more fruitful, I think.

"Perhaps if you win, you can demand I host a foxhunt at dawn. I would be obliged to do your bidding."

"Or I could get you to draw some boxes down from the attic that need sorting."

"Oh, it would be a shame to waste a credit like that on stowage. I was anticipating much more creativity."

"I am thinking of enlisting you for the most menial, sensible, and practical task possible. I do hope I win."

He laughed at her and passed another serve of the picnic lunch-plate Willis had prepared. "I almost hope you do too," he conceded. They had one more animal spotting layover and then headed back to the Hall.

They handed over their horses to the stable-hand and then came inside chuckling with confidence about the tally each of them had acquired. Jeremy nodded soberly as he greeted them at the door. "Sir, Lady Whitmore would like to see you in the drawing room. Miss Hannah's presence is requested also."

"Thanks, Jeremy old man," said Digby. He nodded to Hannah. "See: our adjudicator stands us to attention immediately so you cannot be caught fraudulently adjusting your tallies."

Hannah laughed as he opened the door to the drawing room. "As if I need to resort to fraud! I am very curious to see what you managed on your hunt, and how it compares." She paused as she saw Lady Whitmore sitting in her favourite chair staring out the window. "Lady Whitmore, are you okay?"

"Oh yes. I think so." She sat up straighter and smiled. "I believe you found me napping. Tell me, how did you fair on the tour of Whytehaven's grounds? Are you prepared to reveal your tallies?"

"I do believe we are."

She indicated the occasional table by her chair and they both ceremoniously laid down their opened cards.

Hannah caught her breath. "You can't have that many! Who is the fraud? You must have illegally included any number of sightings that are entirely imaginary. Show me."

Sebastian shrugged, indifferent to the charge.

She picked up the card, studied it intently and burst out laughing. "Lion! You have lost all credibility Mr Digby. There was no lion."

"Humph! The challenge of this game is that we will never know. There are no witnesses to verify the truth of it one way or another. If I noted all my sightings to yourself, I would be equipping the competition. And I do like to win. But to satisfy your scepticism, I will reluctantly permit you to cross that one off the tally."

She scratched it out emphatically. "It is a flawed game. Pheasant? Where?"

"On the ride to the brook. Right hand side near the ridge."

"I only included sightings at our stop-overs. Horse? You can't include the horses. We were riding them."

"Believe they have fur."

"Fox? We didn't see any foxes."

"Ahh but I did. Near the oak tree. Just for a fleeting second. But there were no limitations on how long the sighting had to be. It still counts. And on that basis alone, if you won't allow the lion, I should be declared the winner as I caught a fox on this foxhunt."

"I was distracted by the need to ride a horse."

"I believe the challenge is all about focus: horse or no horse. You are looking at a very observant, skilled hunter. It cannot be denied!"

"Hannah dear, ask Willis to bring some afternoon tea. Now that we have established that Mr Digby is the winner of this frivolity, let us have a cup."

When she returned, they sat down, and Digby began to speculate what he would extract as his prize. Lady Whitmore was not really in the spirit of the occasion and seemed to disappear into reflections as she gazed out the window. As they finished tea, Hannah stacked the cups back on the tray. "M'Lady, are you sure you are feeling quite well? You seem quiet."

"Hmm. Perhaps. I received some correspondence today and I would like to talk to you both about it."

"Oh, dear Lady Whitmore, you should have said. I trust all your family is doing well?" She put the tray to the side and sat down.

"More than adequately, it seems. Sebastian, you know your older brother has returned from the colony. It seems he has decided to take up residence here at Whytehaven Hall."

"But he laid aside any claim until you passed on. Roderick told everyone he was going back; that he didn't want it. That's why he left to start with," Sebastian declared.

"Well, perhaps I did the discourtesy of not dying conveniently. Anyway. This is the current information. I am not dead. And he is moving his wife and family into Whytehaven Hall. In the Spring. He expects me to vacate by mid-February."

"Vacate? M'Lady where would you go?" exclaimed Hannah.

Lady Whitmore turned to Sebastian and passed him some sealed correspondence. "This letter was included and addressed to you. It provides some additional information. If you would open it, Sebastian, I would be grateful."

He ran his finger over the seal and unfolded the paper. He scanned the pages... twice. And then he sat back and laughed. "Ooh! What a hoot!"

"Come, Sebastian, now is not the time for your flippant denial of a situation. What does it say?"

"Aunt Biddy... I... am..." He lolled back and laughed some more.

Hannah stared between the two. "Did you say Aunt? Lady Whitmore is your *aunt*?"

"Aunt? Well, no... not technically... not really. Oh, but now she is so much more. Now she is my *gaoler!*"

"Sebastian is the son of my cousin Beth, who married the Earl of Digby when his first wife passed on. He has two other sons. Beth's health was quite infirm when Sebastian was little, so he spent a lot of time here at Whytehaven. Digbys are also related to my late husband. Cousins. Their eldest son is the heir apparent of Whyhaven since my husband died."

"You grew up here at Whytehaven Hall?" Hannah asked incredulously.

"What does the letter say, Sebastian?" she repeated firmly.

He went over to the drinks cabinet and poured himself a glass... and brought one back for Aunt Biddy. He sat down and closed his eyes, trying his very best to hold his mirth in check. "This letter is from his lawyers. It says... it says that

Father has changed his will and adjusted the allocations of the inheritance. He wants it enacted immediately now that Roderick has decided not to return into exile. Part explanation of this unexpected family reconciliation is that Roderick made sufficient money to adequately address Father's debts… and that apparently gives him license to do whatever he wants. They have allocated me a portion of the family estates. So instead of the esteemed role as the family pauper, I am now a man of property."

"How is this a problem? It sounds like a good thing."

"The condition in me taking possession is that you, Aunt Biddy, become my curator. Or guardian, warden, manager, fairy-god-mother… the specifics are not clear, but as my god-parent, you are to accompany me to the new residence. While you live, I am to provide you with a home and that home must be with me."

"Pish-posh and twaddle, Sebastian. That isn't reasonable. You don't want to live with an old duck like me."

"If I choose not to take occupation under these terms, my existing allowance will be axed. Your pension, that was agreed on after Uncle Eddie died, will also be terminated. They both will be diminished over the next five years anyway: from 'little' to 'nothing'."

"These terms seem rather restrictive. Do they suppose that you will become self-supporting?"

"That may be the least of it, Aunt Biddy. It seems the intention is to cut us off entirely. The place is… well… the property is in the colonies. Actually: Australia." And he sat back and laughed.

5.

"Australia!" they both exclaimed in unison.

"With Roderick home, it says they need me there to oversee the operations of the farm he established. As if anything I've ever had to contribute was considered worthy! Anyway, even though he's been back for a couple of years, suddenly it is deemed urgent to have someone there. To that end, they are signing the deed over to me. I now have property in Australia. How ludicrous is that? For the term of my natural life! They might as well put a bullet in my head or a noose about my neck. I am a condemned man."

Lady Whitmore handed her glass to Hannah. "Pour the man another drink. He has had quite a shock. And myself."

Hannah got up but her hand shook so violently that the decanter rattled against the glasses. She put down the carafe and leant hard on the cabinet trying to calm herself. Sebastian came over and led her back to the lounge and sat her down. Then he went to the tray and brought back three drinks and passed them around. Hannah held up her hand, but instead of protesting she took the crystal tumbler and quickly swigged at the amber liquid. She paused, looked at her glass and then proceeded to scull.

Sebastian quickly reached out and took the glass from her hand and put it on the table. "Whoa up there, Miss. Steady on. You'll pass out on me if you keep that up."

She stared at him wordlessly and took a deep breath. And another. Then she picked up her glass from the table and took another drink. A pain in her chest started to get bigger and bigger. She had no idea what to do or how to stop it. The room started spinning.

"Miss Hannah? Miss Hannah! I would really like to apologise," said Sebastian firmly. As she turned to him with a frown, he tossed the contents of his glass all over the front of her dress.

She gasped and stood up. "What on earth are you doing?" She inhaled sharply and dabbed at the mess on her dress with a kerchief. "What sort of profound thoughtlessness or malicious intent inspired that?" she snapped at him.

Sebastian sat with his empty glass in his hand and leaned back and half smiled. "Is there not a third option? I feared you were going to swoon. I am a firm believer prevention is better than cure, and I am not the sort to pinch smelling salts under your cute little nose."

"That is outrageous! The colonies are the perfect place for your barbarous behaviour!"

"So, you concur with their sentence to deport me? You would also slam the gavel? And you didn't even have to take me to the Old Bailey to do it."

"Children! Stop!" Lady Whitmore sighed. "I will have to send you both to the garret if you don't behave. This is not solving anything." They turned in their seat towards her presiding there with a matriarchal grim set to her mouth, their eyes wide with surprise. Before they could say anything, she softened her tone. "This state of affairs is a pretty pickle to be sure, and it impacts each of us in a profound way. We need to support each other, because it is evident, we have been discarded by family… such as it is. You, Hannah, are included. So don't go behaving as if you are not part of this."

"Yes M'Lady." She sat back down; her damp dress forgotten.

"Aunt Biddy, what do you mean?" asked Sebastian. Lady Whitmore pursed her lips and said nothing. "What does she mean, Hannah?" repeated Sebastian, turning to her with his eyes narrowing.

Hannah lifted her chin. "I may not be family, but this news affects me also."

"How?"

"When you met me, you said my name is the perfect designation of cooks and maids."

"So? It was a line-in. I wanted to talk to you."

"Well, it may have been your peculiar way of introduction, but ironically it was more accurate than you supposed. I am no glamorous lady. I have no genteel family connections. I am not here because your Aunt is my social patroness, but because I am her companion and carer… in service. When you leave, I am out of a job, and I am out on the street."

"That's rubbish. She will still need care. If we have to go, you come with us."

"I am just here. Don't talk as if I am not in the room," said Lady Whitmore.

"Tell her, Aunt Biddy. Roderick might be the prodigal black sheep returned to the fold. It might even be, that in the eyes of Father, he radiates ethereal rays of sunshine from his less than glorious backside; but his despicable behaviour does not run in the family like the colour of our hair. You will keep your job."

"It's Australia! Why would I want to go to Australia?" exclaimed Hannah.

"Why would any of us want to go there? We don't, but we may not have a choice. We have to find out if what they propose is contestable. I suspect that there will be no grounds for challenge. I also know that Father's lawyers will have written this up so that unless we comply, we will need to pursue the lifestyle of market-square beggars, which, as far as I am concerned… is not my inclination either. I fear this is going to be the preferable course of two very bad options."

Hannah blinked and then suddenly shook her head with a chuckle and a smile and sipped her drink again.

"How can you suddenly find a sense of humour when things look so very grim. What is it that amuses you so?" he said bewildered.

"I have just realised that is the first sensible, non-superficial, completely level-headed assessment I have ever heard you offer about anything. You said that whole thing without jokes or asides. Perhaps there is hope for you yet, Sebastian Digby; even if that hope lies in the outback paddocks of Australia."

6.

"Is this the pouting of one who didn't win?"

Hannah shook her head bewildered. Everything about this man defied her experience. "No. I don't know why you still want to hold me to the rewards of your silly game."

"Oh, you offend me! It was not silly. I would anticipate, Miss Hannah, that if the tables were turned, you would be as willing as any to extract your prize. I entirely expected you to be a more gracious loser."

"Sebastian, there are so many more serious matters to consider than whether you get to collect the spoils of an amusing game. Are you not consumed with what you need to do to get ready for your new endeavour?"

"I have lived in rented quarters my entire life. All my worldly goods, apart from my clothes, have generally been the chattels of various estates – of which I have no claim. I could swag my entire earthly possessions into a seaman's bag and be done in an hour. That hardly constitutes the preparations of months."

"Would you not aid Lady Whitmore in her preparations then?

"She has you. And Aunt Biddy is an independent, head-strong, capable woman. If she needs my help she will ask."

"But…"

"Or perhaps you are using this as an excuse to avoid paying your debts."

"It was just a game."

"Well, that depends on who you ask. A card table is merely a game, but I have seen men go to a duel over the winnings and losses in that arena. I take my winnings seriously and I won't be put off."

Hannah sighed. "It seems entirely too frivolous given the changes that are afoot. Very well. What service can I render for you? What do you wish to claim as your prize?"

"I am entitled to two services… but let me start with the first."

"Declare your preference then."

"I would like you to accompany me on an early morning hunt. At dawn. You suggested it and I thought it just too good an idea to pass."

"I believe it was your idea, and as long there is no tally to go with it, I will do it. But I will not be caught by you devising a way of accumulating more obligations from me."

"Oh, Miss Hannah, you assume I am entirely too clever. Such a thought never entered my head. Very well. No tally, but to compensate you will have to assemble our breakfast picnic basket. And no horses. We will walk."

"Walk?"

"Yes. So much more to see when we walk. There is a basket in the kitchen pantry that can be carried on my back. My Uncle Jonathon brought it back from Asia and I have wondered about that basket my entire life. It looks like a lot of fun."

Hannah shook her head and turned to go as she heard Lady Whitmore's bell tinkle for her attention. She glanced back over her shoulder. "I will talk with Willis and ensure we dine well enough for our outing. It seems she would do anything for your lordship."

He grinned and acknowledged. "She's a good sort. We go way back."

Hannah blinked and hurried on with her duties as Lady Whitmore's bell rang again. Yes. She kept forgetting he had spent enough time here at Whytehaven for it to qualify as his childhood home. Lady Whitmore was losing her estate, but he was also losing the home he grew up in.

The next morning, just as the horizon started to pale with the light of dawn, Hannah wrapped herself up warmly and went down to the kitchen. She lit the candle and finished packing the hamper. When Sebastian joined her, she adjusted the leather strapping to his height. Then they set off, Sebastian setting a strong pace across the courtyard in the stillness of morning. The rooster crowed and the birds in the hedgerows were stirring with their glorious waking morning song. He whistled the mimic of a birdcall.

"I didn't pick you as a morning person. You are utterly too chirpy." observed Hannah as they walked out over the little stone bridge, the morning mist lying low across the watercourse.

"So, you think my life involves habits far too slovenly to incorporate a brisk morning hike?"

"I just assumed you would be more comfortable with mild evenings by a drawing-room fireplace."

"I suspect you don't really know me at all, Miss Hannah. I find this type of arrangement perfectly satisfying."

"How is it then, that in the time I have been with Lady Whitmore we have not crossed paths here at Whytehaven? Why do you not visit? Did you not enjoy your time here?"

"This was my childhood haven, just as its name suggests: full of adventure and fun. These *Feathered or Furred* hunts are a Whytehaven tradition that Uncle Eddie always had time for. I suspect Aunt Biddy rescued me on more than one occasion by having me here between school terms. There was so much energy in this place back then. It's like a mausoleum now in comparison. Who wants to be buried alive in a crypt? I can't be judged for dodging better memories of a livelier time."

He stopped and paused and pointed to a squirrel scurrying up a tree. "That's one," he said victoriously.

"You promised no tallies."

"But if it is a shared tally, we both win… that would be a most fortuitous twist on the game. We would each get to elicit an act-of-service from the other."

"No tallies. At all. Shared or otherwise."

They walked around the lake and sat on some logs looking over the water. Every so often another bird or animal drew their attention. Sebastian took off his backpack and arranged their breakfast picnic. "This is the perfect spot to watch the sun rise." The sky melted into a pink and mauve haze softened by the mist rising off the mirrored water. Some ducks swam through the veiled light creating ripples on the surface that circled out to the edge of the shore. Then a brilliant streak of gilded light nudged over the horizon as it flowed across the autumn countryside in a liquid golden flood.

They said nothing for a long time. Sebastian looked over at Hannah and said with a smile. "You wondered yesterday if I have been thinking of my new venture. I was not entirely straightforward: I have been thinking of this quite a lot... particularly one aspect of it."

She stirred curiously. It seemed he was offering a confession that was not based entirely on jesting. "Which part of the venture has your attention?"

"You. Tell me you will come with us. Aunt Biddy needs you."

"The main reason Lady Whitmore employed me was that she was often alone here at Whytehaven Hall. Her stroke was very mild, and she has no lingering problems. Since it is a requisite that she lives with you, she will no longer be alone."

"Me? I am as useful as a fifth leg on a saddle horse. You can't think that is a good idea. She needs someone sensible. You said you needed the job."

"I do. I just don't think I need a job in Australia. I am hopeful I can follow up some contacts that will offer the same sort of arrangement as I have here."

"Okay. Okay. You allow me no recourse. It seems I have to come clean. There is another reason."

"There is more?"

"There is." He grimaced as if he had a tooth ache. "I... I'm not sure I can do it. I need you there to bring some sense into the idea. To stabilise me. To keep me sort of real..." Why couldn't he just declare what Aunt Biddy saw was obvious right from the very beginning? He was in love.

She laughed, clear as the morning air. "You think I am your ballast? That is neither flattering nor sensible. You don't need me, Mr Digby. You might think you do, but you have more than enough resources within you to see this through. You can do it."

"See that. That! Right now, I believe you. I believe I can do this. Self-doubt is gone. Confidence has risen. Now I am a colonial boy, and nothing has changed except you said so."

She shook her head and laughed again. "You make it sound so believable."

"I need to be convincing. I tell you what! Marry me. Come to the colony as my wife."

"What? No!"

"No? Why no?"

"No, because I don't want to marry you."

"You don't?"

"It might seem inconceivable to you, Mr Digby, that some consider marriage a serious thing. It takes more than a handsome face and good humour to create a suitable proposal."

"Ahh, so you have a list. A serious list. This tally will be much more interesting than *'Feathered or Furred'*. So, you concede I am handsome, and I have an amiable nature? That is a pretty good start. Of course, you are absolutely correct: being grotesque and ugly with bad humour would be a terrible beginning to marriage."

She smiled and shook her head. "I really don't have a list."

"Tell me your list and I will help you find your soul mate."

"No! I don't have a list, and even if I did, it would be a private thing."

"Hmm. Let me see. Handsome. Tick. Good humoured. Tick. What else would be on your list? A title! Perhaps you require a title. I have a title. Of sorts. Kind of a meaningless, nothing type of tag though… and I don't think it actually gets me in anywhere… except perhaps an obligation to donate more to the church."

"Sebastian, I don't care for a title. You forget my station. That would be a presumptuous item to put on any list, even a hypothetical one."

"But it couldn't hurt. Sounds impressive to be married to some sort of Peer, be it a Baron, or an Earl, or a Viscount. Why not?"

"I don't require a title."

"Handsome. Tick. Good humoured. Tick. Title – bonus tick. What else? Property. That would be a good one. Oh, what do you know? I have property now. No idea what it looks like, whether it is productive or whether is it even respectable. But it is land that has extracted my brother at least some sort of income: enough for him to return with a sufficient wad to deal with Father's debts. But I suspect something changed if he abandoned a potentially golden goose. That is very uncharacteristic of Brother Roderick, so I am suspicious that it will not be anything like the hallowed grounds of Whytehaven, no matter how much he talks it up."

"You really have so little information about what it is you are obligated to?"

"I will collect the books, logs, and ledgers after Christmas. I suppose there are sheep… or cattle… or goats… or perhaps badgers. Actually… kangaroos! I believe Australia has kangaroos." He chuckled and shook his head.

"Again, you are right: I really have no idea. But back to you… you distract me. What else?"

"What else?"

"What else is on your list to be an eligible suitor for the glamorous Miss Hannah Johnson?"

"I said I don't have a list."

"Of course, you do, because you told me I don't qualify. I can only be eliminated on the basis of a list."

"Well… I believe I want love. My parents had that, and it made everything that was hard and intolerable over the years, softer and more tolerable together. Yes, I want love."

"I agree. I have watched my father barely able to stomach any one for a lifetime because he lived in a loveless house, scrambling and fighting over money or the lack of it. Love is essential."

"Oh. So, Mr Digby has his own list."

"Ahh yes. I do. Would you like to hear it?"

"Sure…" she shrugged.

"Beautiful. Good dancer. Kind. Generous. Sensible. Accomplished. Good humour – can't forget that. I don't care for the title either. We agree on that. Can travel. And love. Must have love. That is my list."

"So why would you ask me to marry you? It is obvious you were not serious."

"Of course, I was serious. A marriage proposal is right up there with *Feathered or Furred*. A very serious matter. Although I didn't realise at the time you didn't meet all the items on my list. I was deceived, so that invalidates such a proposal straight away."

"Deceived?   On what matter don't I meet your standard?" And then she smiled as she realised, she had been set-up to ask.

"You won't travel… to Australia. I have no intention of having a wife whom I have to leave behind here in England. That would entirely not meet my purposes in a spouse… at all."

7.

Jeremy walked into the drawing room. He was followed by short man who bowed deeply. "Lord Ernest Gromley, M'Lady." He gave a sort of shuddering sigh that ended in a snort, as he rose.

Lady Whitmore stared at his sideburns, barely masking her consternation. "Lord Gromley, you seemed to have found your way to Whytehaven Hall after all. Were there no other more pressing invitations at your disposal?"

"My dear Lady Whitmore; an invitation from yourself and your esteemed protégé is my most pressing duty to honour." He spoke loudly with a lisp as if talking over the hubbub of a music hall. In the hallowed sanctuary of Whytehaven's parlour it grated uncomfortably.

"Well, I have not seen either Miss Johnson or Mr Digby this morning. I suspect that they have gone hunting again."

"Digby is here? Oh? You said they have gone hunting *again*?" he said loudly with a frown. "I would have thought this type of occupation would not be to Miss Johnson's taste. But it is a fine tradition of the aristocracy..." His voice quickly faded as he coughed with a snort and stared at an empty chair.

"Lord Gromley, would you like to take a seat?"

He grunted his thanks as he flipped his coat tails out of the way and sat. He gazed at the tea-tray that stood empty by Lady Whitmore's side-table. He shuffled and cleared his throat.

"Have you eaten breakfast, Lord Gromley? Will I call for our maid?" And she rang the bell for Willis.

47

"Well, M'Lady, thank you! I have come quite a way. Some breakfast would be entirely fitting. I will have three eggs, poached, with a side of liver and mushrooms... it is the season of mushrooms... and a thickly cut slice of toasted bread, buttered both sides. And, of course, a pot of tea, drawn for exactly three and a half minutes. That is the optimum time for pleasant cup of tea. Four is too long. Three is too short. I always find breakfast to be the most enjoyable meal of the day. I know some who do not esteem it so, but to their discredit, I always say."

"No doubt you do," said Lady Whitmore quietly. She was wondering whether she could send Jeremy to the garret window to send semaphore signals announcing grave danger to the pair returning from their excursion. It would offer the humane kindness of avoiding the Hall until the coast was clear. Or... would she throw them unhesitantly into this den of irritation to save herself? Gromley sidled his chair up to an occasional-table and flicked his kerchief onto his lap in anticipation.

He dabbed his lips and slurped his tea in the daintiest way. Lady Whitmore quickly decided she no longer had any qualms restraining herself from signalling a benevolent warning. Now she considered how to message for help in the manner of a vessel floundering on coastal rocks. She studied the buttered crumbs sitting on his side-burns, coated in a smear of gravy and wondered how it was possible they didn't fall. She watched them with fascination as they jiggled while he spoke around his full mouth of chopped liver. Even food didn't offer any relief from his monotonous tirade.

"Do you like to hunt, Lord Gromley?" she asked when he paused.

"Well, I do like a good game of whist. Are you a card player, Lady Whitmore? I am sure a lady of Miss Johnston's accomplishments would be a capable player. Perhaps we could all play a game when she returns. I always find a good game of cards the most enjoyable way to pass the time of the day. I know some who do not esteem it so, but to their discredit, I always say."

"I'm sure you do..." She sighed with relief as she heard Sebastian and Hannah laughing in the Hall as they made their way inside. Jeremy took the basket from Sebastian's back and ushered them into the drawing room.

Hannah bobbed a curtsy. "Oh, M'Lady you have company. Please excuse me: I will go and change my dress." Lady Whitmore looked at Hannah curiously as she left the room in a bustle. Her skirt was damp and muddy around the hem. Her hair was windswept, her cheeks blushed and her eyes bright.

Sebastian eyed the occupant of the chair, noting the teapot and crumbs. He smiled disarmingly as he sat down and crossed his legs. "Good morning, Gromley! I can earnestly say this is an unexpected diversion." Sebastian didn't even pause to notice that when he was around Ernest Gromley his need to speak "earnestly" always increased in frequency. "It was a wonderful morning out on the wild fells and dells of Whytehaven."

"Hunting? Did you shoot a covey or two?" asked Gromley as he lurched forward with a sudden burst. Lady Whitmore jolted whenever he spoke.

"Well, I could earnestly say that... the prize I was looking for got away. Didn't aim my shot well enough, apparently." Aunt Biddy looked at him quickly and studied his masked face.

"Humph! Well, I find just a little more time to sight the shot generally reaps its rewards with a higher count at the end of the excursion," Gromley pronounced emphatically.

"That sounds entirely barbaric."

"Oh no; I always take a boy to snap their necks. Very quick."

Even Sebastian could not suppress a smile as he saw Aunt Biddy's lip curl in revulsion. "Always very sensible to have children do our dirty work. Entirely civilised," he said.

Aunt Biddy cleared her throat. "Sebastian, would you like a cup of tea?"

He smiled and without hesitation leant forward to pour a clean cup from the tray setting. "Oh, I don't think I would miss this for all the tea in China."

Gromley stared at the liquid in his cup in surprise. "Is this Chinese tea you are serving? I actually prefer the imported Indian blends for the most refreshing cup of tea. Our beloved Empire is known for its excellence in tea. I know some who do not esteem it so, but to their discredit, I always say."

Sebastian turned towards him in fascination. "Are you a connoisseur of tea leaves, Gromley?"

He nodded and almost blushed bashfully. "Well, I do consider that I have a very discerning palate for this esteemed English delicacy."

"Have you ever tried the Malayan blends? Another corner of the Empire. I have heard the Marchioness from one of the Empire's provinces gives the most convincing appraisal of its rich flavours and drawing qualities. The Malays have a rather unusual way of "pulling" the blend as they pour. Of course, I doubt you have had the opportunity. It is a very rare experience… and usually only for those with elite privileges."

"Malaya, you say? That wouldn't have been the wife of the Marquis De Barona?"

"You know *them*?" he asked incredulously, and he saw Aunt Biddy in his peripheral vision gag on her tea and quickly put her cup back on her saucer.

"Well, yes. The Marquis is a very good friend of my father's admiral… of the merchant navy. So, I think it is very possible I have had that sort of tea. My memory serves me that you are right and indeed it was very refreshing."

Hannah entered the room and caught the glint in Sebastian's eye. She curtsied as the men rose. "Mr Goonley here was telling me earnestly he has experienced the exquisite flavours of Malayan tea. How about that?"

"Gromley. *Our* name is pronounced *Grom*-ley."

"There is more than one of you? That is an unforeseen circumstance," said Sebastian under his breath before sat back taking another drink of tea.

Hannah extended her hand. "Lord Gromley, it is an unexpected pleasure to have you visit. What brings you so far from your home?"

"He has come for tea. Malayan tea is best. Indian tea is tolerable. Chinese tea is not to be borne."

"Really, Mr Digby, is there so much to be discerned in a single pot of tea?" she said looking full into his face with a tilt to her head.

"Oh, to be sure," Gromley interjected, as he had the distinct impression that he was being bypassed in a conversation on which he was an expert. "I find a good exchange and interesting company is always enhanced by these exotic blends."

"I wonder which are the erotic blends? That sounds more interesting than this current menu," Digby surmised under his breath as he took another mouthful of tea.

Hannah tried very hard to stay composed. She had no idea breakfast tea could be controversial and attempted to determine how best to divert the conversation. Lady Whitmore took a breath and put her cup on the tray. "Lord Gromley was telling me that he is an accomplished whist player."

"Whist?" they both said in unison.

"Whist is a diverting way to get to know each other," he said significantly in Hannah's direction.

"By playing cards?" said Hannah doubtfully. "This early in the morning?"

"I am sure Miss Hannah is an accomplished player," Ernest earnestly affirmed. "…at any time of day."

"Capital idea!" exclaimed Sebastian. "There are four of us."

"Miss Hannah would make a suitable partner. Mixed partners are always preferable," Ernest earnestly affirmed again.

"Oh Gromley, how right you are: mixed couples it is. And my friend, I noticed you have very discreetly acknowledged that both you and Miss Hannah are accomplished Whist players… so it would completely tiresome to have two experienced players playing against us amateurs. You can partner Lady Whitmore, and Miss Hannah can limp along with me."

"I do not want her disadvantaged," said Ernest earnestly.

"I do not think Lady Whitmore will be disadvantaged," countered Sebastian. "Give your experience more credit, Sir."

"It is merely a game, so we can have some fun without taking it too seriously," offered Hannah as she suddenly had visions of both of them drawing pistols in a dual over the outcome. And she almost cringed as she became aware how much she sounded like Sebastian Digby in that moment.

They rearranged the seating and brought out the deck of cards. They dealt and played the cards. Sebastian and Hannah won the majority of tricks in the first round. "Well, Gromley, Hannah's tutorage is paying off this morning. What an excellent suggestion of yours that we play mixed couples. I can't wait to see what other diverting suggestions you have as a man of experience."

"Well, I do say that keeping company need not be tedious, but rather open to all forms of entertainment."

"How right you are, Gromley. How right you are!" And he sighed an exaggerated sigh of contentment while Gromley smiled a coy schoolboy smirk in Hannah's direction.

Hannah cleared her throat and stood to her feet. "Lady Whitmore, I will go and inform Willis that we have company for lunch before we embark on the next round."

Sebastian stood with uncharacteristic helpfulness. "I'll come with you... to hold the door," and before she could protest, he was opening the door and bowing as they exited the room.

As they walked to the kitchen, Sebastian grinned. "So?"

Hannah shrugged. "So? What?"

"How does the list go?"

"No! He is not here for me."

"Well, he is not here because he is genuinely concerned for Aunt Biddy's improvement in whist. The list needs to be considered."

"Oh... I... that's ridiculous," she laughed.

"Handsome?" he asked, and she didn't respond so he continued. "Undeniably, those whiskers are a fashionable effort. But it gives him a brutish sort of look in my mind. Is that to your taste?"

Hannah cringed.

"Hmm," he said, "the panel is undecided on handsome."

"Good humour? Well, he does go to a lot of effort to be agreeable in a bland, mind-numbing sort of way, but whether that is *good* or not is also uncertain. Is it not? Hmm. I thought so.

Title: He ticks that item. But I will remind you that you have asserted that is an irrelevant point.

Property: He is in line... so as Lady Goon-ley you would manage your own household... whenever his parents pass on. I *have* heard his family has the reputation of longevity, and his grandparents on both sides lived to three-hundred and seventy, deaf as doorposts. So, you may actually die before them and never occupy on your own terms."

She smiled at him and shook her head. "Sebastian, stop it. He is here as Lady Whitmore's guest." She didn't feel annoyed. After she spoke with Willis briefly about the menu, she turned to Sebastian. "You know I am amazed. All that fuss about tea. It is an art-form for you, isn't it? To expose another's peculiar foibles."

"Only when they are ridiculous. He doesn't even make it hard. It becomes rather tedious though if the survival of boredom becomes the only challenge." Sebastian paused, and then plunged ahead. "Miss Hannah, from my objective and impartial point of view, I fear that Goon-ley is floundering to make the grade on your list. I did better in the tally and didn't get over the line. So... I think it is unfair that you give him hope."

"Hope?"

"Hope that you would happily accept the honour of being Lady Ernest Goon-ley."

"He can't seriously think..."

"I earnestly think that Ernest earnestly does. He is not the brightest candle in the chandelier." Sebastian leaned in and whispered conspiringly. "There is a simple solution."

"There is?" Hannah internally groaned by how complicated this morning had quickly become.

"Oh yes. So simple. He is not aware that you are... Hannah of the 'maids-and-cooks' ilk."

"That is what this morning is about?"

"Absolutely. But if you want to let him down gently... graciously lift the cover on that. He will fly."

"I actually suppose if he was truly interested in me, that would be of no matter."

"Perhaps, but his parents would never stand for the controversy. Test it and see. If I am wrong, I will humbly apologise, and dance the polka at your wedding."

"*That* I would like to see... the apology," she quickly clarified.

He raised his brow and opened the door as they both plunged back into the whist circle with cordial smiles pasted on. At the end of another round, it was still Sebastian and Hannah's game, so Gromley pushed for another set to vindicate his self-appointed status as Whist player champion. Hannah stood to her feet and apologised meekly for leaving before the next play. "M'Lady do you need any help to freshen up before lunch?"

Lady Whitmore frowned and considered her. "Perhaps... if it is not too much bother."

"No bother at all, M'Lady. It is, after all, what you pay me for."

Gromley physically lurched, and then he smoothed his brow and relaxed. "Very generous of you, Lady Whitmore, that Miss Johnson is bestowed an allowance during her stay with you."

Lady Whitmore stood, and carefully adjusted her shawl. It was enough of a pause for Hannah to cough delicately. "Oh, my, Mr Gromley. Please do not insult Lady Whitmore so. It is not an 'allowance', but appropriate wages for a full day's service. Lady Whitmore would never deny another what is their due."

Lady Whitmore then cleared her throat and nodded firmly. "Let's be on our way then, Hannah. The men can amuse themselves with anecdotes of hunting and other gentlemanly pursuits while we are gone." As they walked to the stairs, Lady Whitmore titled her head. "You must realise, you just closed that door very firmly. You could have successfully solved your income concerns for the rest of your life with that particular drone. As queen-bee you would have had a very healthy hive to your credit."

"Oh, M'Lady, you know me better than that. It was a test. Sebastian suggested it. I thought he was exaggerating a little, but perhaps not. Mr Gromley did seem disturbed."

"I very much doubt we will have to worry ourselves about the other setting at lunch. But no matter. We have dodged a conversation debating white-meat versus game-meat. I am entirely relieved."

"If he was wrong, Sebastian said he would apologise."

"Hmm. I doubt he will need to humble himself so." They reached the top of the stairs. "Since we have gone to the trouble for a special menu, go and put on a pretty tea-dress. We will have a pleasant lunch regardless of whether or not we have company."

"Lady Whitmore?"

"Yes dear?"

"Thank you for not treating me like the Help. You are an exceptional woman."

"Pish-posh and twaddle, Hannah. I am just partial to the idea that you accompany me to Australia. I may even offer you a raise or resort to other forms of bribery and corruption to persuade you."

"I am flattered that my service means so much."

When they returned downstairs the dining table was set and Sebastian was lounging unperturbed in a side chair fiddling with his pocket watch. Mr Gromley was nowhere to be seen. Sebastian regarded her changed dress with approval and raised his brow. Hannah met his gaze, and he stood up and came over to her. "You did that with such sublime elegance, I could not feel more proud. It is like you are my protégé."

"You take too much credit, Mr Digby," she responded, unperturbed by his flattery.

"Goon-ley asked that I pass on his regrets at being unable to stay for your esteemed invitation. For which I am relieved. I could not have endured another moment with that imbecile. I would note that it took fourteen minutes and thirty seconds for him to take his leave. Fifteen minutes would have been entirely too long. He did last about eleven minutes longer than I supposed, so I will humbly apologise for underestimating his stamina."

"Mr Digby, you are so very harsh!"

He shrugged. "Perhaps. But I am not wrong. I trust you do not feel disappointed that your efforts to preen and prettify will go unwitnessed by the earnest Mr Goon-ley." He held out his arm and escorted her to the table.

She blushed and shook her head. "Not at all. My efforts were not for his benefit."

He raised his brow and looked at her with a smile as he held her chair. "Well, it does need to be said. So, in his stead I will declare it earnestly: you look so *very* beautiful."

8.

They sat after dinner in the candlelight. Lady Whitmore had her usual reading lamp turned up and her eyeglass adjusted as she settled in for her evening reading. After a bit, Sebastian looked directly at Hannah. "I am running out of time you know. I might need some help."

"Ah-huh!" said Hannah as if his confession meant she had caught him doing something quite inappropriate. She tied off a thread on her embroidery piece and rethreaded a new colour.

"You say that as if my asking for help is a character flaw," said Sebastian.

"It is not at all a moral failing. I am just surprised that you are at the point of exposing yourself to someone's assistance."

"Miss Hannah, I fear that you expose a whole lot of undesirable traits in my nature that have been happily concealed my entire life. That is on you, not me. I was quite content."

"I did not suggest that asking for help is undesirable. In many respects, it is very sensible to be able to realistically assess our limitations."

"Ahh. See. There it is again: the enduring persistence of being sensible. Do you do anything that is not driven by pragmatic logic and sensibility? Which, now, actually helps me a great deal in my dilemma. I have been pondering on what second service I could get you to render as my prize. The week to extract it shortly expires."

"Oh Mr Digby. You take being frivolous to untamed heights. Do you not have more serious matters to atten...? Oh, but no. Of course not."

"I think this is completely serious. It is the notion of balance. Your judgment is that I take nothing seriously. I would suggest you take everything far too seriously. Together we can offer each other some balance. I have not thought about life so seriously since I have met you. And I am on a mission to help you enjoy some of the meaningless aesthetic aspects of life that have no sensible or practical applications at all."

"I cannot see how your mission to enhance my silliness is at all to my benefit, or yours."

"That is exactly my point, Miss Hannah: there is no point. It is just for the pure exhilaration of being alive. So, with this in mind, for my next service I would like you to play the pianoforte for me. No practical accompaniment in the service of others; just unsullied music that has no need to be anything other than a beautiful melody filling the atmosphere and which is gone in the moment."

Hannah sat still and stared at him with a frown. In a bizarre way, that seemed like a very rational argument in the defence of music. "You assume, Mr Digby, I could render such a service. How do you know I can even play well enough to deliver such a request?"

"Because logically, it would be very sensible for you to be able to accompany ladies in their solos, children in their dance lessons, and gentlemen in their boredom."

"Are you confessing to being bored?"

"Not even assuming I am a gentleman. Besides, the servants talk. They say you are very accomplished. This is a service I render for you. See, I cannot be all 'malicious intent' if I would take my prize and sacrifice it on the altar of service to another."

She wondered how she could extract herself from this obligation without seeming petty or pouting. That didn't seem likely, so she stood up and walked over to the bookcase and opened a folder of music. "For someone who is claiming to be self-sacrificing, Mr Digby, you seem entirely too smug."

"For someone who is paying out a legitimate debt, you seem entirely too reluctant. I guess we achieve balance once again."

Hannah went to the keyboard and opened the cover. She sat down and arranged the sheets. She hesitated a moment before she gently coaxed the soothing lilts of a Bach prelude from the ivory keys. It was an elegant piece in its simplicity. Lady Whitmore rested her book in her lap, absorbed completely in the moment, listening with her eyes closed. When she finished, Hannah shut the cover gently and resumed her seat on the sofa and wordlessly picked up her handiwork project. Sebastian studied her face with a silent smile of appreciation and said nothing. When Hannah rose to attend to Lady Whitmore at the end of the evening, she came over and quietly said, "Mr Digby, thank you."

"You thank me?"

"Thank you for not carrying on with banter."

"What could I say? It was perfect in every way. I was wrong about that."

"Wrong? What do you mean?"

"The music. I said it would be gone in a moment. But I was wrong – so very wrong. It has lingered, and dallied, and tarried all evening. And it has been exquisite." He nodded, excused himself, and retired. Hannah was immersed in thought as she looked at his retreating back, and then gently took Lady Whitmore's arm to assist her to her room, to settle her for bed.

9.

The carriage door opened, and Hannah quickly took the rug from Lady Whitmore's knee and held her hand as she alighted. She readjusted the muff around Lady Whitmore's wrists for warmth and held her arm as she hobbled up the front entrance. As they passed the doorman, Lady Whitmore groaned. "Please take my weight, Hannah, I feel very frail. Walk slower, Girl. This is not a derby race-meeting. Have some consideration!"

Hannah frowned and said nothing apart from, "Yes, M'Lady."

"Take me to my suite immediately, Hannah. I am exhausted from the trip," she said as she handed her travel-wrap to a hovering coat-boy.

"It is to be expected you are tired, M'Lady," said Hannah gently as she guided her along the hall to the staircase. "It was a long and gruelling trip."

Lady Whitmore huffed and puffed, groaned, and wobbled all the way to the guest suite. Then, as Hannah closed the door behind them, Lady Whitmore stood up straight and strode over the lounge. She sat down and patted the space beside her. "Sit here, Hannah. I need to explain a few things."

"Yes, M'Lady," she said with raised eyebrows.

"I have requested a trundle cot to be included here in the guest suite, so you will be staying with me. You may find I will become exceptionally needy over the next few days. Just be patient with me – there is a purpose."

"A purpose?"

"Yes. I wanted you to come to this Digby Christmas, not because I particularly want to soil your experience of the holiday, but I feel that it may help if you witness this household in action. It really is a performance in the proportions of a Shakespearian tragedy."

"Lady Whitmore, it seems you can be quite theatrical yourself. I have already committed to staying with you until you board your passage. Of course, I would attend you during the Holy Season. Who is this going to help?"

"Me – to start with. Take this as fair warning: this week is not going to be easy. But it may make more sense to you why he is the way he is."

"Who?"

"Sebastian. I am hoping that you will use this information and reconsider my request to extend your employment with me… abroad."

"To Australia? My employment with you has nothing to do with Sebastian."

"Of course, it does. I have to live with him. That means you will have to, also."

"Oh, M'Lady, I had not considered that! I am not sure I could do that."

"Pish-posh and twaddle. Of course, you *can*. You are not sure yet, if you are willing."

"Did you know he asked me to marry him?"

Lady Whitmore looked away and tried to sound indifferent. "Oh? And what did you say?"

"Well, I didn't take him seriously of course. But I think he might have gone along with it if I had said yes."

"Probably."

"So, did I do the right thing?"

"In putting him off? Oh, my dear, how would I know? You are best to gauge whether it is right for you to marry or not. That is not my place to say. I've seen arranged marriages in action and I am very convinced that the new trend of couples choosing for themselves is entirely an improvement."

"But wasn't your marriage to Mr Whitmore arranged?"

"Of course. Given the option, we would have made the same choice all over again. It was entirely marvellous from the first time it was agreed we would meet. But I have also seen it go the other way. I've seen gentle and beautiful people plummeted into hell because of family economics and brutish politics. I don't want that for you or Sebastian. But just because you want to exercise that choice and decline to marry, doesn't mean you can't come with me as my companion. I will need your assistance during the passage. They say it is not easy… and I am not getting any younger. Just tell me you will reconsider."

"Yes, M'Lady, I will reconsider. But my mind is fairly set."

"Yes, Hannah. I know. You are a girl who knows her own mind. Now, for this week… there are some Digby Manor rules."   Lady Whitmore very succinctly laid down the expectations. "There will be no friendly banter between staff and family. There will be no fraternising between staff and family. You would normally eat separately; sleep separately; breathe separately… not even the same air should be consumed together. The exception to this, of course, will be permitted because my extremely fragile health demands that you sleep here in my rooms. I will also require breakfast served here. When that door is closed and locked, we can go back to normal. This is our haven. Out there, life is segregated, and you are invisible. You will wear that uniform and behave as starched as your pinafore. Whenever I hold up my hand like this: it means that you are to come running to my side to attend to whatever petty and unreasonable thing that I need. I have also requested a wheeled chair... so that we can at least get away once a day and look around the grounds. It will mean that either you or Sebastian will need to push it. Probably that will be you because when others are around, the fraternising rule strictly applies. You cannot be seen to be just keeping company. Your presence must always have a practical purpose."

"I can do practical... I think."

"It will also help if we are consistent about my maladies. The main concerns are my headaches. So, an urgent mission at least once a day... maybe twice... running down to the laundry or scullery to get clean towels or bowls to soak my poultices, may be convincing. We might even add some screaming and crying from behind these doors."

"M'Lady, is this really necessary?"

"Oh yes. Look as worried and as frazzled as you can. If you need a break, you can come back here and clean. I have already intimated that I require my rooms to be kept pedantically immaculate to accommodate my fragile health. I am expected to attend all lunches and dinners... and to socialise for a short time in the evening before retiring."

"Does Sebastian know these rules? Will he conform?"

"He knows the rules… and does his best to flout them at every turn. You must not give in. Your face is a mask of servitude. Always."

"That sounds a bit more complicated."

"This is for your own defence. Please trust me on this. I will have an afternoon rest between one in the afternoon and dinner, which is served at six. I will spend my rest-time here in these rooms. I will have no visitors, under any circumstances, while I am resting. It is your job to keep them out. If you have to be rude and severe do not hesitate. Sebastian, of course is permitted to come at any time. This doesn't apply to him. Christmas will be an all-day affair from the Church service in the morning."

"Oh, M'Lady. This does sound… difficult."

"It is. Believe me. Any questions?"

"Yes, M'Lady. What happens if we get caught?"

"Caught?"

"Well… caught fraternising?"

"Let us just say that it is better if we don't."

"Yes, M'Lady."

"Perfect."

10.

Hannah stood behind Lady Whitmore's chair at the dining table in her pinafore and starched white apron. She was unexpectedly grateful that she could stay invisible. She looked straight ahead and did her best not to look directly at those seated at the table, adorned in extravagant layers feathers and fur, and imagined playing a game with Sebastian. In her peripheral vision she added to the feathered and furred tally in her head, but calculations were cut short by the impatient grunting of Roderick.

Every meal was demeaning and outrageous. Lord Tyndale Digby sat at the head of the table and bellowed at the incompetence of the staff. Lady Digby tried to placate his temper, until she was offended, and then it was her turn to berate their unsatisfactory service. Roderick sat beside his father, stoically deaf to his ranting, and impervious to the pleas of his wife, Lucinda, who often had a swoon or had to urgently attend to the children in the nursery. Sebastian's other brother, Bellomy, drank too much and offered his opinions too loudly, making jokes – usually at Sebastian's expense. Hannah saw him pinch the maids and clout the coat-boys when they came too close. It was like observing Hell through some sort of spiritual looking glass.

Together, Lady Whitmore and Hannah had devised a strategy to remain suitably incognito; camouflaged in a belittling ecosystem. At least once during the meal she would signal for Hannah's attention. "Yes, M'Lady," she would say, "What is it you require?"

"I require you not to be so dull! Pour me another drink." If she poured wine, she would demand water. If she poured water, she would demand wine. There were variations on this theme: bread with or without butter, soup with or without cream. Hannah was amazed how easy it was to devise means to be scathing. She would flush, and attend to Lady Whitmore's unreasonable demands looking harassed, keeping her presence unobtrusive as possible. She noticed that her unquestioned acquiescence would elicit a grunt of approval from the patriarchs sitting at the head of the table. She also noticed when Sebastian would leave the table with a great deal of grunting of his own, disgust oozing from every pore along his very handsome jawline. She had not yet seen him survive to the end of dessert.

Hannah wiped down the table and dusted the mantelpiece. When she heard a knock at the door, she answered it assuming it would be Sebastian. She had systematically discouraged every other occupant of the house, so that they avoided Lady Whitmore's rooms, rest period or not. It was not Sebastian who stood there, but Bellomy. She quickly closed the door, but he shoved it open.

"You were expecting someone... and it wasn't Aunt Batty," he said suspiciously as he pushed his way in.

"Excuse me. I am cleaning the rooms," she said quickly holding up her feathered duster.

"The old Bat is still downstairs. How is it that her maid doesn't have to attend her but gets to dust the furnishings at her leisure? I heard humming," he said accusingly.

"I am working." She stepped back as he leered at her and grabbed her apron.

"I have work I need to attend to."

She stepped back again and then slipped her apron as he reached out again and caught it. He was left holding it, his face getting closer to the shade of the red wine on his breath.

"There is something about you, Miss. Something that don't quite ring true. I'm reckoning there is…"

"I don't know what you are talking about!"

"Sure, you do. I'm talking about 'Bastian and Batty. They both be too tight with a maid to be proper. I think my pathetic, loser little brother, has got an eye for his old batty aunt's maid. Well, I've got my eye on you too. He can't even pick a real lady." He threw down the apron and circled around the chairs.

"I don't know what you are talking about!" she gasped, backing away.

"It isn't any wonder they are *deporting* him. Him getting the colony property… that's *not* recognition 'cause he carries the Digby name. He is not getting what I deserve. They didn't overlook *me…* who is next in line. Nooo… he's being *transported…* in the most respectable way possible for a proper respectable family. They just want the embarrassment to go away. So, they are putting him on a galleon."

"I have no idea what you are talking about. I am *just* the maid." She looked around in panic and backed further away.

She tried to circle back around to the door, but he cut her off, eyeing her with a sneer. "You are the maid: that is for certain. But I'm thinking it is not just *"just"*. Just not sure… *just* how far it goes."

"I need to attend to Lady Whitmore's remedies. They are due."

"I have a remedy," he said as he cornered her and grabbed her arm. She shrieked and Bellomy pulled her in, clapping his sweaty palm over her mouth. She squealed and struggled and kicked. He knocked her to the ground. "The maid has a temper. That isn't respectable." And he grabbed at her pinafore. She kicked and cried; her eyes wild. He struck out and hit her hard across the jaw. Her head spun and she fell backwards, knocking her forehead on the leg of a side table. She heard something crack and blacked out.

She came to, lying on her trundle bed. She could sense someone standing over her and she struggled to sit up. She felt her shoulder being pushed down and she thrashed again. "No! No!" He backed right away, and Lady Whitmore came into her line of vision. "Hannah! Dear. Lie still. You hit your head."

"Oh, M'Lady. You are here… I need to…" She groaned and reached up and felt her forehead where a tender raised lump had appeared. She lay back against a cushioned roll, her head thumping.

"I know. I know. Well, the proverbial cat is out of the bag now."

She closed her eyes and opened them again, trying to understand what they were saying. "What do you mean?"

Sebastian moved in beside his aunt. "She means that my disgusting no-good brother has uncovered the pretence. There is the slightest sliver of a chance that he is not entirely stupid; just a malicious, vile reprobate. He disgusts me!" A growl rose from the pit of his diaphragm, and he paced around the room.

"Bellomy? He… I tried…"

"Hush Hannah. We don't have to talk about it now."

She lay still for a moment and then sat up. "No, I need to. What happened?"

Lady Whitmore swallowed and looked at Sebastian who nodded. "Very well. Tomorrow is Christmas Eve but it means the plan has now changed somewhat."

"How?" Hannah shook her head and tried to focus.

Sebastian interjected. "Meaning you don't have to play the ridiculous compliant maid anymore! My brother seems to think that he has conjugal rights with any staff in the house! No – don't worry he didn't, but I had to make you untouchable." His voice calmed and he looked to his aunt for reassurance. She nodded. "I'm sorry. But we are now betrothed. It was the only way. Aunt Biddy confirmed it. That is her ring," he said pointing to Hannah's left hand. She held it up and on her finger was Aunt Biddy's beautiful ruby and diamond ring.

She stared at it in disbelief. "What? Engaged?"

"I had to explain Bell's broken jaw, and his very black eye. It seemed appropriate."

"Oh."

"The upside is, that because I have connected the family to the very basest levels of society, we are banned

73

from Christmas dinner... or any dinner. You can thank me for this later."

Lady Whitmore's face was grim. "So now... all we have to do is stay out of the way. The Holiday Programme will not be disturbed just because of us. So, as Sebastian has intimated, we are barred from social events until after boxing day. Then Sebastian will be given his records, and we are on our way."

"But you said we are engaged? Truly? Does this mean I have to marry you? Don't I get a say?"

"Betrothed... for at least four days. Father would normally demand such an engagement be terminated, but because we are being exiled, he doesn't really see the point of exposing the controversy. Once we leave, we are practically dead and buried anyway. So, I can't even have an engagement that he would care enough about to dismiss. He still manages to suck the life out of everything... even an inappropriate betrothal."

"You said we were engaged just to rile him," she observed.

"Well, that was a side benefit to be sure. Primarily it was so I could legitimately slog my contemptible brother. To the rest of the family, it just proves that I do not fit their despicable world and the colonies option is better for them and appropriate for me."

"Oh Sebastian. I am sorry." She felt woozy and her head wobbled ungainly like it was too heavy to hold. She lay back down.

"But on the positive side, I got to live my dream."

She opened her eyes. "What do you mean?"

"I dreamed of being engaged to you… so now I am. Even for a couple of days."

She shook her head. "I don't understand…" Hannah gaged and rolled over, and he grabbed her head and a basin just in time, as she heaved and was sick.

Hannah vomited all through the night with varying degrees of intensity. Sebastian stayed all night and left once he knew she was out of any real danger. By morning the servants rumoured she was pregnant; the Digby's refused to acknowledge she existed; and the doctor called in by Lady Whitmore diagnosed a "brain commotion" caused by the hit to her head. He also declared that there was an accompanying "nervous hysteria" brought on by their unconfessed forbidden love and the need for pretence with Sebastian's family. That combination had put the girl in grave danger, and it was prescribed that she be confined to bed.

Hannah thought that notion sounded quite irrational for a man with a doctor's bag, but she lay there quietly trying to take it all in. Sebastian put no weight on the peril imposed by a "nervous hysteria", but he did wonder what it would be like to have Hannah collaborating in a forbidden and passionate love. That idea made him raise his brow and smile, more than once.

11.

On Christmas morning, the entire household, including the servants, rallied themselves for a seasonal evacuation in a fleet of carriages for the Yuletide Church service. The Digby congregational booths were, on special occasions, dusted off and occupied with an appropriate amount of clanging silver coinage. The servants got to stand in the upstairs gallery of the church and generally enjoyed the birds eye view with the pigeons. They whispered their observations on the various hats and muffs and coats worn, and they noted very carefully who-looked-at-who during the carols.

When Sebastian came to their suite, Hannah sat quietly on the lounge after attending to her morning ablutions. The powders that the doctor had left were to be taken in mitred amounts if the pain became intolerable. Her head ached less and she declined them.

"Well!" Sebastian announced. "Everyone has left for their Christmas duties at the parish church. The beauty of this means we have a two-hour window of reprieve from their intolerant bickering. So, it is my vote that we abandon all the usual traditions and go on a Christmas hunt. There was a light fall of snow last night so there is an entirely different world to be explored. Are you up for that Aunt Biddy?"

"Goodness, why would I go out in the snow when there is a perfectly good fire in the hearth? I have some Christmas reading I need to attend to," she said as she opened her Bible, "So you two go along. Take the wheeled chair so that

Hannah does not overly exert herself according to the doctor's instructions. Look after her Sebastian. She is reconsidering coming to Australia as my companion, so I don't want that jeopardised. She is very much part of my survival plan."

"And mine..." said Sebastian under his breath as he gathered the chair from the corner.

"I can walk," Hannah said, as he navigated the chair to her side.

"I would not dare suggest you couldn't. This attempt to abide by the rules is a rare deviation from my pattern, but it has been recommended enough times for me to consider the merit of this reform."

"I... well, perhaps it is sensible that I support this uncharacteristic inclination to attempt compliance."

"Very sensible. Come. Let's go outside while we can. Soon this place will be swarming with unwanted Digbys. There is such a small opportunity... and regardless of the occupants, this estate has a rather spectacular garden."

Hannah rose and wavered ungainly. He steadied her, adjusted her coat, and guided her to sit in the chair. Before she could protest, he had wheeled it out the door, waving to Aunt Biddy through the hall. He stopped at the top of the stairs, swept her up into his arms and carried her down the stairway. She looked too shocked to protest and he grinned. "Doctor's orders," he said with a wink. He put her down in another wheeled chair positioned at the base of the staircase, tucked in a rug and spun it around to go outside using a side entrance that had been adapted with a ramp.

He slowed down and leant forward speaking in that familiar conspiring whisper. "We go this way: this is a special treat. In winter the garden transforms into an incredible mystical planet – straight out of a child's reader."

Hannah almost sighed in relief. She was thankful that something of the familiar Sebastian had survived this family homecoming. In an effort to distract them both from the halls-of-horror that awaited them when everyone returned, she boldly dived into a bout of *'Feathered or Furred'*. "Robin!" she whispered as she spotted an orange breast on a crystallised twig.

"Squirrel," Sebastian pointed as a tail disappeared up a tree trunk, and he gently steered the chair along the path, his tread crunching the ice.

"Jay."

"Cardinal."

"Sparrow."

"Starling."

"Unbelievable!" said Hannah holding her breath. "I thought every little creature would hide from the cold."

"I will confess a secret. One of the stable hands fills up a feeder. It is around the back of this grove. Can't be spotted unless you know where to look." He stopped in an alcove off the path.

"Oh, Sebastian, it is a beautiful! A pristine world of wonder!"

He took the rug from her knee and helped her up. "Let's sit just over here. Hang on... slippery." He guided her around the corner, and they sat on a bench bundled in rugs.

He grinned. "I've always thought these little topiary trees could be lollipops on a stick."

Frosted hedgerows surrounded their nook like Willis' sugar-dusted pastries; sculptured bushes stood like ice painted toffee apples; miniature shrubs lined up like sweets. "Yes! We are sitting in a Christmas box of treats – filled with every imaginable delight."

"That garden over there is not surrounded by a low hedgerow, it is a sweet bowl of pudding topped with an ornamental cherry." Sebastian glanced her way. "This little corner of the garden is one of my earliest, purest memories… something my mother shared with me when I was little."

Hannah stayed fixed on the scene before her. "I'm glad you have that memory. It is a shame that things have changed so much."

"What?" He laughed. "Oh no. *She* is not my mother. She married my father as soon as *my* mother died. She probably used the church the same day since it was already booked for the funeral. I was about ten years old and sent straight back to the Academy. We never saw eye to eye."

"Lady Digby is not your mother? She is not Lady Whitmore's cousin? Oh, that is a relief. She is certainly not a mistress of the finer things of life…" She stopped and apologised. "I'm sorry. This is not what I expected."

"You can admit it. Anything you say would probably be criminally polite."

"I'm so sorry Sebastian. I am grateful you have held yourself to a different standard than what is here."

"Was it not you who told me that we get to choose? That we alone are responsible for our own choices and direction?"

"I did. I thought I was encouraging you to a positive direction, but I did not see to what degree you have already accomplished this."

"Perhaps the bump on your head has given you clarity."

"Or perhaps I prided myself on humility when I had no idea of the extent of my arrogance. I am so sorry, Sebastian. Forgive me."

"Of course. You were not to know. Biddy and my mother were close… more like sisters than cousins, but Biddy refused to visit here for obvious reasons. Christmas was the exception. If attendance wasn't mandated no one would have turned up, and a poorly attended Christmas threatens one's social reputation. You had to show in person for the distribution of allowances or any endowments to social committees. So, you can see: a Digby Christmas was unbearably loud, competitive, the more obnoxious flattery one could manage might mean a bigger cut of the donation pie. I have no nice memories. Mother's health became a very good reason for me to stay with Aunt Biddy during term breaks. Sometimes Mother would come to Whytehaven as well. Mother's health was always blamed, but I can acknowledge, now, that perhaps it was her attempt to protect me in her very powerless life."

"Did you feel protected or palmed off?"

"Oh, definitely protected. Biddy's husband Edward, 'Uncle Eddie', he was great. Had a wicked sense of humour.

And confidence! He was a tower of strength. And his brother, Uncle Jonathon, of the wicker-picnic-backpack notoriety, he was the same. We didn't see him very often, but he used to tell the most astonishing tales of adventure. The last time I saw him was for my tenth birthday; he went overseas on another adventure after that... who knows where. The Americas, I think. I like to imagine him climbing the Andes Mountains or gliding a canoe through dark Amazon jungles. Oh yes, I felt protected... and appreciated... and a favourite. Anyway, after Mother died, Biddy insisted we keep the same routine at Whytehaven. It is the only place I think of as home. I was twenty when Eddie died; it was like a light went out at Whytehaven. I tried to forge a place for myself in other places. Never really managed it though. Always assumed Whytehaven would be forever available to me. To be sent away from here... I don't care about this, but knowing I'll never see Whytehaven again: that rips me up. I've no idea how Biddy can be so calm about it."

"Perhaps she isn't. But perhaps she is doing what she has always done: protectively filling the gap for you. It is evident that she loves you like a son."

"Yeah. Dear Biddy. She is the one consolation in this debacle. It is unfair that she is being punished for caring all these years. That is what it feels like... a way to make her pay for loving me. But no matter how I try, I can't imagine what sort of mess we are walking into. So, I don't blame you, sensible Hannah, that you will not buy into it. Given a choice, I wouldn't either."

Hannah took a deep breath. *Well… about that…* She looked out over the blanketed garden and wondered how she could suggest it.

He noted her silent pause. *Hmm,* like he said: *sensible, but none the less disappointing.* "Hannah, I want you to give Biddy her ring back. It was the one that Uncle Eddie gave her."

"Oh! Yes! Of course! I wouldn't dream of keeping it."

"Since it is Christmas, I have a gift for my betrothed." He pulled from his pocket a small lace trimmed handkerchief. He handed it to her.

She took it and unfolded it cautiously. Inside was a striking, unusually set ring with an ornate turquoise and enamel feature on a turquoise band. "Oh Sebastian, this is so beautiful!" She stared at it, mesmerised by its design. "I wonder where it comes from. It looks so foreign… exotic." Then she suddenly looked up. "Are you giving me this so I will give Lady Whitmore her ring back? You know I will do that."

"It was my mother's. And even if we are to be betrothed for less than a week, this was always to be given to the lady I asked to marry me."

"Oh! I can't keep it. No, I won't. It must go to your bride!"

He shrugged. "Well, you wear it… and give it back when you resign from being my affianced. It adds credence to the betrothal."

She laughed and shook her head. "Okay. Until then. You are amused I have ended up engaged to you. Even if it is a pretence. You are a man who likes to get his own way."

He shrugged and didn't look offended. She sobered and caressed the ring. "Sebastian. Thank you. Thank you for defending me."

"Entirely appropriate, given you are going to be my wife." He wasn't talking metaphorically.

"Very well. I promise. I will keep it on while your family is present. The theatrics of this house continues. Right now, we are dreamily engaged." And she leant forward and kissed him on the cheek.

He froze for a moment feeling her breath on his skin; then quickly thawed and stood up. "Agreed. Well, we had better go back to Biddy's rooms. The priest does not take long for his Christmas liturgy. It is typically something of a speed-read. We will be invaded again very soon by Digby barbarians, so let us go forth and fortify our stations.

12.

Sebastian sat on the lounge and grinned as if he was eight years old again, cooking up mischief. "You know, the greatest form of revenge will be leaking out subtle hints that we are having a fabulous time in here without their input or consent. It will drive them to distraction. Even the servants will be sent crazy," and he burst into a hilarious bout of laughter.

Hannah grinned at his uproarious comical display. "I am going to suggest that 'subtle' is not your forte."

Aunt Biddy sat her shaking her head. "That is just the sort of ridiculous reprisal that Eddie would devise," she admitted as she allowed herself a fairly loud chuckle.

"What can I say, Aunt Biddy? He was the master and he tutored me well. He would say to me, *'Bastian my son, choose a comeback where no one can throw a rulebook at you. Avoid the logical argument and watch how they handle being speechless. It is worth the effort when they have no recourse.'* There is no law or logic that says it is wrong to enjoy Christmas Day. It is a festive day designed for merrymaking... so let us do that." And he laughed again as he walked closer to the door. "Miss Hannah, would you like to join us for a game of cards?"

"What game can we play with just three? It is an odd number that is never accommodated." She shook her head and had no doubt that if Sebastian said he wanted to play cards with three, three would be the exact number required.

"Whist with a twist. It is a diverting way to pass the time, I always say!" he chuckled with an earnest lisp. "Three hands dealt, no partners and whoever wins the trick, gets to nominate a category for any person to share a story: Christmas, birthdays, weddings, or funerals. No sad stories though… that is the rule."

"Then why include funerals?"

"Oh, because there is a wealth of absurd funeral moments that should not be excluded from any family folklore. If you can't think of a story, and you break the flow of anecdotes, then you must declare up front a personal foible and share a ridiculous observation about yourself. The penalty is an act of service, of course. But regardless of what is chosen, whether it is a *story* or *a study*, there must be copious amounts of laughter for our audience outside."

"You assume we have an audience."

"Oh, we definitely have an audience. It is like one of those shadow pantomimes behind the screen, where the audience believes what they see, but it is not at all what is going on."

He pulled the chairs up to the table and shuffled the cards and dealt the hand. Then he cut the deck. "Hearts is trumps."

"That is the appropriate suite for a newly engaged couple," observed Aunt Biddy. And they all burst out laughing.

"Keep those observations coming, Aunt Biddy: no need to wait until you are nominated."

"Oh, this is entirely too amusing to wait," she countered and again they all laughed at their charade. Every so often Sebastian would pull a face and tilt his chin towards the door, and that would send them laughing again, as they heard the scurry of mice at the door.

The stories flowed; the pauses between the laughter were few. Sebastian trumped his hand. "Yes! I get to nominate again!" He turned to Hannah. "Miss Hannah, share a wedding story if you would please."

She didn't hesitate. "I would like to declare that instead of a story, I want to offer an observation."

"You would break our run? But we have done so well: story after story for countless hands. Very well, observe yourself as the study. What folly would you expose?"

"My foible is that I am choosing a course of action has no logical foundation. It doesn't make sense, and yet it seems I am determined to go ahead with it. My ridiculous observation is that I have decided to stay in Lady Whitmore's employ. I cannot leave you. Not now. If the offer remains open, I would very much like to come to Australia with you. Please. That will be my act of service."

The silence became loud. Lady Whitmore put down her cards with a shaky hand. "Oh Hannah, you sweet thing. This is not the prize from a card game, but the most precious Christmas gift you could offer. Thank you my dear. Thank you!"

Hannah got up and went around to her chair and gave her a hug. "Lady Whitmore, you are as dear as a mother to me. You know it. I cannot stay behind. I have tried to convince myself I could… but it is entirely impossible."

Sebastian grinned and nodded, but his eyes were thoughtful, and he tried to discern if he might be a contributing factor to this decision. Nothing. She didn't even look in his direction. Still and always: Lady Whitmore's companion. He cleared his throat and went to the drinks cabinet and brought back a tray with three glasses. "You are entirely right. Ridiculous to the core! But as foolish as it is, this is indeed a cause for celebration! My mother had a saying that seems an appropriate toast for an occasion such as this. Raise your glasses: to unbroken circles!"

"Unbroken circles!" they chimed, and they toasted and laughed as the mice went scurrying at the door again.

13.

Sebastian opened the door to the library and stepped back so Aunt Biddy and Hannah could walk in. He followed. They stood in front of his father's desk like school delinquents brought before the study-master for reprimand. They were all dressed for travel, and Aunt Biddy made sure she had on her largest hat, and longest fur.

His father scowled. "What are *they* doing here? Grief Sebastian, can't you even do business without women holding your hand like some nursery milksop?"

"Aunt Bridget's presence is obligated since she is a mandated feature in my future. It is entirely appropriate that she and my fiancé witness signing these documents."

"Par! You are such a disappointment! Your mother would be disgusted by this display of feeble impotency. Pathetic! Show some grit man. Lord knows you are going to need it in that cesspit colony. At least Roderick saw the sense to come home."

"I am here to collect the documents I need for that 'cesspit'. And to say goodbye."

"And good riddance! Your face is the shame of the proud Digby name."

"Where are the documents?"

He threw a sheet onto the desk. "That is the deed. Sign under our names on this transfer... and there."

Sebastian took the time to scan the document and signed with the quill sitting on the desk. He docked the pen, and his father waved the paper impatiently to dry the ink, rolled it up with the deed, wrapping it in a leather document sleeve. He tied it, tossed it back onto the table and dismissed Sebastian with a wave.

Sebastian eyed the leather roll but did not move. "The letter indicated there were ledgers, registers, and logs. Where are the records?"

"What records could there be? That colony is a filthy suckling piglet! It is a stain on our glorious Empire. It is not England boy, even if they dare claim her as their Sovereign. They do things differently there. Now get off my estate!"

Aunt Biddy's mouth was grim as she turned and guided Hannah back through the door. Sebastian picked up the deed and followed, his eyes dark with rage. They passed Bell flirting with a chambermaid on their way to the front door. His jaw was bound, and his left eye was puffy and bruised. He turned his back as they passed, focused on the giggly, plain-capped face in front of him who pathetically soothed and stroked his wounded pride. They did not see Roderick or Lucinda. They could hear Lady Digby yelling at the kitchen staff. Life at Digby Manor went on as usual without them.

The coachman had loaded their travel trunks. As they went around the circular sweep of the drive, Sebastian looked out the window at the garden coated again in a powder of snow. Suddenly he lifted his stick and rapped the ceiling firmly. The coachman pulled the horses to a stop. He jumped out and slammed the door behind him, striding out across the grounds leaving footprints in the snow.

Aunt Biddy grimaced and then nodded to Hannah who bundled her out, adjusted her muff and coat and took her arm. "Do you know where he has gone, Lady Whitmore? Is he okay?"

"This place is poison, and he is suffering from its toxin just now."

"But where is he going with such urgency?"

"To say goodbye to his mother. She at least would be respectful enough to wish him well."

"Oh Lady Whitmore. What can I do?"

"You are like a tonic to him, Hannah. You counter the poison. Just by being here, you are what he needs."

They stood back and watched as he leant over her gravestone. It was plain and dull, standing diminutively beside other ornate Digby monuments that were ostentatious in their grief. He leaned heavily on the simple curve of the frozen stone and felt the strength of her love and the coldness of her abandonment. This was his goodbye. It seemed this was the only good thing he was leaving behind. The rest he was taking with him, and in that he could not be sad. He stood up. There were no tears, or smile, or witty quip. He turned and silently walked back to the carriage alone, his hands deep in his travel coat pockets. Lady Whitmore and Hannah followed behind, saying nothing. When they arrived back at the carriage, Sebastian opened the door for them, aided his aunt on the step, offered his hand to Hannah, and squeezed it ever so slightly before he silently took his place beside them. He tapped the roof of the carriage and it rolled on towards Whytehaven Hall. They had six weeks to vacate.

14.

Lady Whitmore stayed in their cabin for the most part. She sold some personal items and scraped together the passage to upgrade to two cabins, so they could avoid the cattle-hold accommodation in steerage. Most days, even if the weather was not fair or the waves gentle, she would have Hannah escort her to the upper levels. They would walk slowly and take a few laps around the deck. On these excursions they would meet Sebastian or talk to someone about the progress of the travel and the nature of seafaring. Most times, Lady Whitmore would return to the cabin and insist that Hannah take a turn about the deck with Sebastian in the fresh sea air.

Hannah learned he had befriended the captain and the first mate. He had met farmers who were relocating as 'free settlers' and relayed their opinions that the prospects the colony offered were more positive than the accounts he had been given. They believed the scanty resources in the settlements offered opportunity for the entrepreneurial.

Sebastian's boredom could not be alleviated with an invitation to the captain's stateroom once a week. His listlessness drove him to go looking for the farming books he had pilfered from Uncle Eddie's Whytehaven library. Reading, if nothing else, would fill the very long and silent hours. A reasonable side-benefit was to try and learn some of the jargon of rural life. For a socialite with no useful trade to his history, the idea of farming was entirely intimidating.

So, he went on a hunt with one of the deckhands to the stowage hull, by-passing the steerage passenger bunks, smelling of stale urine, body odour and vomit. They searched through the stowage allocated to the Digby/Whitmore passage, pulling aside the sea-chests that had been filled with Aunt Biddy's personal and household paraphernalia. There were trunks with clothes and linen and family heirloom china. Items of furniture were restricted to family inheritances that belonged to her personally rather than chattels of the estate. The rest of what was needed was to be purchased on arrival. He found the books and extracted them. As he was restacking the box, he came across another smaller sea trunk, battered in its appearance. It had a number of shipment labels stuck to the side but rather unexpectedly, they were marked 'Mr Roderick Digby'. The label on the lid was crossed out and his misspelt name was scrawled in its place. Sebastian shuffled it into the aisle and inspected it curiously. There was no telling what it contained exactly but it was intriguing enough to have it taken to his cabin.

He closed the door to his cabin and lifted the lid. Inside was an untidy assortment of books and papers. He pulled out the first book and opened its cover. It was a journal; irregular entries were signed by Roderick. He flicked through the pages and then went to the next book. That was a ledger. He put them on his cabin table and rifled through the loose papers. He closed the lid and went straight to knock on Aunt Biddy's cabin.

When Hannah opened the door, he stepped quickly inside without ceremony. "Aunt Biddy the most remarkable find has been uncovered!"

She looked him over. There was an excitement in his eyes that had been dull and listless for weeks. "The diversion sounds like a relief. Tell me."

"I went looking for the books from Uncle Eddie's library, and I found a small chest, with Roderick's name on it. I think it contains the ledgers we were promised. It is a mess, and I expect the records are sketchy, but this offers the best clue of what we are dealing with."

"Where do you think it came from?"

"No idea. I can only imagine that a sympathetic someone was told to dispose of it and chose instead to dump it in amongst our luggage before we left. I need Hannah to come and help me sort it. It is going to be quite a project."

"Me? I know nothing of ledgers and accounts."

"I just need an ordered mind and some sensible direction. If you can't offer that, an extra pair of hands will suffice."

Hannah hesitated. She was entirely bored, and this was the most interesting thing that had happened since they boarded. "Where?"

"In my cabin."

"I can't go to your cabin."

"Why not? You are my betrothed. You still wear the ring."

"I didn't give it back because you suggested it might be protection on the vessel from frustrated sailors and wandering passengers."

"Well, you don't need protecting from me. Come Hannah. You are curious and want to help. We can't do it anywhere else."

"Of course, I am curious… very much, but I do not want to cast doubt upon your reputation."

"My reputation means nothing here anyway. I'm a castaway, drifting aimlessly towards an eternal black hole called Australia."

Hannah frowned and refused to be amused.

Lady Whitmore stood up. "Come on young lady. I am craving distraction even if you are not." And she picked up her stick and her book and walked to the door.

Hannah looked startled and grabbed their shawls as she closed the cabin door. "Very well, since Lady Whitmore will accompany us, it will give us something interesting to do," she said as she followed them to Sebastian's cabin. The space was small, and Lady Whitmore sat in the only chair. The bunk was unmade, and Hannah quickly smoothed the covers.

Sebastian frowned. "It is hard to sleep neat when the bunk is six inches too short. More comfortable than a hammock I suspect, but only just. You are not my maid, so don't clean up after me."

"I'm not doing this because of a pedantic need for tidiness. We need a surface on which to sort papers," she said.

"Well, okay then," he conceded and opened the trunk. He took out a couple of journals and piled them on the desk. "I can review the books at leisure; it's the loose sheets that we need to sort." Sebastian glanced uncertainly at his aunt who nodded firmly. He took a breath. "All right then. This docket is for household items: flour and salted meat. Do we need this?" he asked doubtfully.

Hannah stood up and looked over his shoulder and took it from his hand. Biddy sat unmoved and opened her book and began to read.

"We are not determining its value as yet. Just creating some sense of order," Hannah said with more confidence than she felt. As he passed sheets over, Hannah placed them in dated order and a number of piles started to appear.

The correspondence caused the greatest interest, and it was harder to categorise. They would read them together and raise their brow at the picture that started to emerge. Letters of demand. Roderick had racked up a trail of debt. Like father, like son. Sebastian would raise his brow at some of the language used and substitute a filtered version as he read. There were records, all be it incomplete, of employed staff. Most supplies were ordered on a bi-monthly basis, so the estate was either big enough to accommodate staff, or remote enough to require it. Poultry had been purchased. Only a few head of cattle. Perhaps they were the diary-maids' department. It was like a dissected atlas-puzzle; they were trying to piece the map together… but there seemed to be more than a few cut-out pieces that were missing from the box. When they looked up Aunt Biddy had gone. The little cabin was littered with piles and piles of paper; the lamp needed trimming and supper had passed.

"Oh! We really did lose track of the time. Lady Whitmore will be worried," said Hannah.

"I doubt it. We are confined on a boat. She can find you if she needs to since she knows where she left us."

"Oh yes. Right." Hannah looked around. "Sebastian? Where are you going to sleep? It is already late, and if we disturb these piles, we will undo all our efforts from today."

"I will grab my pillow and sleep on the floor."

Hannah sceptically eyed the few spaces that were already cluttered with more piles of paper.

"Deck chair?" he offered lightly.

"No! You are not sleeping on the deck! What if a squall blows up and you are swept away?"

"Soo… would you miss me?"

"Sebastian, please don't."

"Don't what?"

"Don't joke about recklessly putting yourself in unnecessary peril. We need you to be safe."

"We?"

"Yes 'we'. Stay in our cabin tonight and I will wake you early so that no one will see."

He grinned. "You are inviting me to stay in your cabin this night? That is scandalous behaviour, Miss Hannah Johnson!"

"It may not be as comfortable as a deck chair, but I am confident it is safer. If I am travelling halfway around the world to companion Lady Whitmore, I am going to make sure that you at least arrive in one piece."

He looked at her amused. "And that was almost a declaration of care. You are becoming attached to me ,Miss Johnson. Soon I will tick sufficient items on your list."

"Sufficient for what?" As if she didn't know. Would he say it?

"Sufficient for you to keep the ring."

She pursed her lips and turned away, "I will let you know…"

In the morning, Aunt Biddy adjusted her sleeping cap as she sat on the side of her bunk and prodded him with her stick. "Why are you lying on my rug like a hunting dog?"

Sebastian rolled over and ran his hand through his hair. "Uhh! Aunt Biddy. Good morning. Hannah insisted."

"She did, did she? Well, this is *my* cabin, and you can go back to your mounds of documents. Take Hannah with you. I can look after myself well enough for today."

"But, M'Lady, please allow me to fetch your breakfast and prepare your tonics first."

"Pish-posh and twaddle young lady. Just because I have hired a companion, doesn't mean I am an invalid. And it also doesn't mean I am not able to hold my own company. You two have work to do, so off you go."

"Yes, M'Lady. If you are sure…"

"I am certainly sure. Come and tell me at lunch that you have sorted out this mess and know what we are getting into. Now leave. I am going to rest this morning for I fear a headache may come on. Please don't disturb me today."

"Yes, M'Lady." Hannah kept her smile to herself as she gently closed the door. She knew the days when Lady Whitmore's dreaded headaches took hold, and she had none of those signs. "Well, it seems it is incumbent of me to be your assistant today."

"I'm starving since we missed supper. To the dining galley, then to work."

They sat and ate. The menu was ship-ration basic, and without embarrassment they dunked their hard-tack biscuits in their cups of tea with the familiar ease of a sailor. Sebastian looked into his teacup and scowled. "I fear this is not to the standard of the fictitious Malay blend. Nor even the humble Indian leaves. I think this is..." He screwed up his nose. "It tastes like the scrapings from the bottom of a peat-bog."

Hannah shook her head at him and laughed. "And you are the one who mocked Mr Gromley mercilessly over his fastidious affection for tea. You are a snob, Mr Digby: a biscuit dunking tea snob."

"Are you reprimanding me, Miss Hannah?"

"You make fun of others... but you have your own idiosyncrasies, Mr Digby. Challenging your attachment to them is a worthy exercise. Perhaps you are not as flexible and open to various experiences as you believe."

"Of course, I am open. I am dunking biscuits in my tea, on a ship in the middle of the Atlantic Ocean, sailing to the ends of the earth. Unless I am open, I do not survive."

"I believe you resent this endeavour. You speak as a convicted man, chained by circumstances. You think only of surviving. That is not open to this venture or the life it could offer. You hate your father and your brother for doing this to you. There are others on this ship who have sold everything for this opportunity. All you feel is sold out. That is very different... and it is certainly not open."

He sat back and looked at her. The smile on her lips had faded. He felt irritated that he could not charm is way out of this uncomfortable moment with a joke. "You have been in the company of Aunt Biddy too long. You are becoming quite missionary in your zeal to improve me."

"Whether you improve yourself or not, Mr Digby is entirely up to you. But I chose to be here. And I would also choose to be with others who want to be here as well. That will tip the scales on whether I end up staying or not. At the moment, this is the question that remains unanswered for me." She rotated the ring on her finger.

"So, you are thinking of staying? Perhaps you have not condemned me to bachelorhood forever?" Curiosity flickered, prodding Hope for signs of life.

"You persist in twisting my words! I said *'undecided'*, Sebastian. I know you could have any woman you set your sights on. Why would you think my refusal condemns you to monkdom?"

"But you refute your own argument. You *are* the only woman I have set my eyes on… and still you refuse me. So, I can't have what I want after all."

She held up her left hand, the ring boldly declaring their fake betrothal. "Do you know why I have not returned your ring?"

"As some pretending shield against brash and lecherous seamen."

"That is not all…"

"You opt to keep it? This is good news… I think." Hope stirred again and fluttered its eyelids weakly.

"You are a good man, Sebastian, but you have no understanding how blessed you are. You are smart, and personable, and you have a knack of being able convince anyone to do anything."

"And yet, I cannot convince you. That doesn't sound to my advantage at all."

"You have insight with other people. Yet I am bewildered that when it comes to yourself – you have absolutely no idea."

"So, this is not a declaration of love… but a confession of confusion? I think I am offended."

"You have no need to be offended, Sebastian. You know I regard you well."

"Just being regarded well by Miss Hannah Johnson is not enough. I need more."

She shook her head. Perhaps he really did have no idea. She stood up and collected the plates. "Today our purpose is buried in a box full of papers. We have much to do… and if we don't get started, Lady Whitmore will be looking for a report after lunch and we won't have anything to offer."

15.

Hannah settled to the task with an attitude of business. Sebastian tried a number of times to illicit a laugh with a joke, but she was determined to keep adding to the piles. As they worked through the trunk, more and more correspondence came to light. Sebastian read every letter, adding his own flippant commentary, mimicking the blatantly abusive tone, or condescending language. "My brother really is the epitome of a people-person," he observed sarcastically. "He is genuinely oblivious to basic human courtesies. His only aptitude is alienating everyone he encounters. It is a mystery to me how he ever got married."

There were loan notes taken out against the land, some even scribbled on newsprint. It seemed he left with the money he secured, and the debts remained. The pile of debt correspondence was quickly mounting. Sebastian sat staring at it as Hannah added another credit note, scratched on brown paper. "For much of my life I took comfort that my pittance of an inheritance meant escaping Father's obligations. I fear we are headed straight into the devouring mouth of a Kraken called debt."

Then he found another letter. Addressed to his father, written by his brother, apparently a draft of the final copy. Sebastian started reading it out, but something caught in his throat, and he continued in silence. His face became graver and darker as he waded through the pages.

Hannah was comparing some documents and did not immediately notice how quiet he had become. When she looked up, she was shocked by the raw disgust that showed on his face. Slowly she stood up and edged towards him. He saw her move and recoiled.

"Sebastian? Whatever is it?"

He shook his head and opened his mouth, but no sound came out. His eyes returned to the letter, and when he finished, he handed her the pages without a word. She held her hand steady, but by the end of the first page she was shaking so much that she lent hard against the ledge that ran along the side of the cabin under the porthole. Sebastian stood up and held her wrist to stabilise her. "Do I need to throw my drink on your dress again?" he said in a hoarse murmur.

"You finish it …" and she shoved the pages back into his chest.

"You can't expect me to read it to you? That's a little unreasonable."

"I want to understand. Just tell me the overview."

He swallowed, and cleared his throat, and tried to sound nonchalant. "Well. Okay. In the interests of keeping your day-dress dry…" His voice crackled and he took a drink of water. He put the tumbler down slowly and cleared his throat once more. "It seems that Roderick came across this fellow by the name of Jack White. He says that he looks exactly like me… or as the case may be… I look like him. He felt it couldn't be a coincidence. He investigated his background from those who knew of him and formed this theory that White was in England about twenty-five years ago… that he and my mother…" He paused and then plunged ahead. "He believes they had a debaucherous affair, and I am the result."

Hannah gasped. But even when he heard her audible shock, by saying it out loud, it seemed to Sebastian a little less shocking.

"Huh. You know... that would make sense. If Father found out while Mother was alive – he would have killed her. I have no doubt. But if he found out now, of course he would launch me penniless into exile. Or as it seems... transfer every known debt to my quarter: to make me pay. I would lay a wager this is why Roderick returned and they have been executing this revenge ever since."

"Are you not outraged?"

"Well... yes... by both camps. But what if she really loved this fellow? You know if that is true, it almost feels like relief. The idea that she had someone who truly regarded her well, holds an element of comfort for me. A pocket of secret affection instead of the incessant misuse and ill-treatment she copped from every Digby. And it would also make sense why Mother would want to protect me." Something almost like excitement rose in his voice. "Huh! This might actually mean I am not his blood! What if I am not his son, or in any way obligated to him? I am spared! All that talk he used to go on about the 'proud Digby name', and all along, I might actually be a White. Oh." He stepped away and sat down on the corner of the desk. He was silent for a long while and he ran his hand through his hair. He looked at Hannah who stood there speechless with a frown. A nervous thought demanded an answer. "Does this controversy mean I can never find favour in the eyes of Miss Hannah Johnson? Does this disqualify me forever?"

"What are you talking about?"

"If all this speculation has grounds, it means I am a bastard conceived out of wedlock, perhaps the fruit of deliberate and intentional adultery."

"Really, Sebastian! You forget I am of the 'maids-and-cooks'. It does, however, make you less entitled to the exclusive gentry's quarter you have been so determined to attach yourself to. Unlike certain tea-sipping gentlemen with sideburns, I hold sufficient character not to condemn a man for his lineage, or lack of it. I believe ancestry is a circumstance quite separate from the issue of our moral fibre."

"But this is a matter of morals. Bathsheba's sin condemned her child to death. That's a damnable offence."

"Scripture also says that a man is responsible for his own sins, not the sins of their father."

"You seem certain. I thought there was a 'third to fourth generation' clause."

"My father was a Rector. He believed whole heartedly in the next portion of that passage… that the *lovingkindness of God shows mercy to a thousand generations'*. Why do we get stuck on four, when God is lavishing blessing to a thousand? When scripture says *'God is abounding in love, ready to pardon, gracious and merciful, slow to anger, and of great kindness'*, I choose to believe that. You are not responsible for someone else's sin… be that the sin of people who loved each other, however illegally, or a father who didn't love you, however lawfully."

He studied her face and tried to discern whether this was the companion of his aunt talking, or the daughter of the Rector. Sometimes he found it hard to know which was her voice. "Hannah… do you think it is possible you could ever love me? Because right now… I am at a loss. I have no legitimate title. It seems I don't even have a legitimate name. The property we are headed for is a sinkhole of bad debt. The things on your list… the cards I thought I held…" His tightly controlled life of intentional insignificance was suddenly blowing away on the trade winds that billowed the sails on their ship.

"Sebastian, do you really not understand? I have told you why I hold your ring, and not given it back…"

"Better to be sensible. There is protection in being spoken for."

"But I hold it still because… because I do not want you to lose hope."

"Hope?"

"Hope that one day it might be more than just insurance against possible danger and disregard on a boat."

"It might?" Hope gasped and took some shuddering breaths of life.

"Yes, it might… I might… But it will not be your name, nor your title, nor your social circle, nor your property, that will capture my heart."

"Do you hide your affection from me? Will you finally marry me?"

She smiled and shook her head. "Not while you continue to present a persona of levity and fickleness, when I know there is more to be offered."

"We could get the Captain to marry us! Or the chaplain, although he is not of the Anglicised faith."

"Firstly, I said 'might'. I am still undecided. But as the daughter of a Rector, *if* we were to marry, it would be in the church according to what my parents would admire."

"You are not only fearless; you are harsh and exacting."

"Why do you take on the role of victim here? You are not. I have not lost sight of Sebastian, the safari guide of Whytehaven fells, on a magnificent and grand adventure."

"Really, Hannah, how can you have so much faith?"

"You told me your offer of marriage was unacceptable because I was reluctant to travel. But regardless of that disqualification, I am here." She held out her hand and slipped off the ring, placing it firmly in the palm of his hand. "Should you offer your ring to me again... do it as a symbol of love, not just someone you are protecting from your vulgar half-brother, or crass sailors and deckhands." He looked at the ring in his hand, stunned. Before he could even take a breath, she turned and ran back to the cabin of Lady Whitmore.

As the door closed, Sebastian called out, "He's not my brother: half or otherwise!"

16.

Lady Whitmore looked up from her reading when Hannah came in. She noticed her breathing was flustered and her face flushed. She quietly rested her book in her lap. "Hannah dear? Are you okay?"

"I think so…"

"Where is Sebastian?"

"In his room, going through the papers."

"Does he not need your help then?"

"I need a break. I may help him again tomorrow." Hannah pressed her hand against her chest and took a deep breath. What did she do? She felt a bit dazed.

Lady Whitmore looked at her hand. "Your ring? Have you lost it?"

"Oh." She inhaled quickly and put her hand behind her back. "No. I returned it. It was not my ring. It was still his mother's."

Lady Whitmore picked up her book and turned the page. "That's a curious point of view," she said without the slightest hint of curiosity. Then she paused and closed the book again. "Are you sure? He made a valid case about the staring mariners."

"My point was about being loved by him, and not creating a false sense of being spoken-for because of others."

"Oh. So, you think he does not love you?"

"Sebastian's entire life has been gifted in opportunity. Working is something he has never had to do with any consistency. I believe he might value things... value me... more if he has to invest some effort."

"Have you considered that if you make him work too hard, he may lose interest and go elsewhere?"

"I have very much considered this. His affection may merely be a shallow infatuation, catapulted into being by a lively polka dance. If he becomes bored, perhaps that is all the evidence I need to realise we have no life together."

The next day, Hannah resumed her role on the floor sorting documents. She never mentioned the ring, but she found herself rubbing her finger, and noticed how empty her hand felt. "Do you think Lady Whitmore knew what was in that letter? She was close to your mother."

"It does seem possible. But she never hinted at anything outside the usual conventions. If she knew, I had no idea she was part of a plot to hide me and my shame away."

"A plot?" Even Hannah was shaken by the idea of Lady Whitmore being a weaver of intrigue. "Are you going to show her the letter?"

"I've thought about it. But Biddy has always rebuked me for carelessness. She's accused me of *'shaming my mother's memory'* more times than I can count. How would she react if I actually slighted the integrity of Mother's virtue? Biddy would be outraged."

"You are not *making* the accusation. You are just presenting what has been made from another quarter."

"She loved my mother. She is not going to stand for such an accusation being made against her."

"I feel like I'm part of a secret that should not be kept from her. How can she know nothing of the true circumstance which takes you both to the colony?"

Sebastian shrugged. "Well, I might not have told you either, except you were there in that moment. Miss Hannah, I consider that we are now bound together by this shameful secret and our lives are forever entwined."

"If you think that disgrace and deception will force me to marry you, that is not the right approach, Mr Digby."

"Hmm. I am increasingly uncomfortable with Digby by name. He never behaved like my father, regardless of paternity. Perhaps in the colony, I'll take the name Whitmore... or some other."

Over and over, they went around and around the topic. Each day they walked on the deck, and turned, and tilted, and scrutinised, and studied the dilemma in a hope that some solution would unfold. They found a small nook, tucked in behind coils of rope and barrels of salted fish where they would sit out of the wind and the sun. It became a place where the smell would cover this secret disgrace. It was a relief to have at least one place where the expectations of society were not imposed on them. Yet, why should he even care what the other cabin passengers thought? After all it was not title or society that had bought them cabin tickets; just a pocket full of money they had scraped together, none too sophisticatedly.

17.

As the trip progressed Hannah continued to insist, regardless of the weather, or even if Lady Whitmore was not feeling up to it, that every day they took a turn about the deck in the fresh air. Sebastian worked on understanding the ledgers, and the books, and started to put to use his expensive education that had been made in the good name of Digby.

One diversion they particularly enjoyed was watching the passenger games on the steerage deck. These competitions offered distraction, exercise, and a healthy laugh. The dances were bold and raucous and overtly flirtatious. They started to become familiar with the regular competitors as they watched. Hannah noticed one teenager dominated the rope-skipping contests over and over. One afternoon, as the girl won a close round, she acknowledged Hannah's hearty applause. Later she came over to the rope that divided the stowage lot from the other class passengers. Hannah smiled at her warmly. "Congratulations. That was quite an energetic effort!"

She bobbed a curtsy. She was even younger than Hannah originally thought, probably around sixteen in age. Her hair was mousey brown, greasy and pulled tightly back off her face. Her eyes were mild, a light hazel, and her chin and nose plainer than seeing her at a distance. Hannah extended her hand. "My name is Hannah. It is a pleasure to make your acquaintance."

"Thank you for your encouragement, Miss. I saw you watching the final round. My name is Penelope. Penelope Toms. But my brother calls me Peggy."

110

"Lovely to meet you, Peggy. My apologies if my spectating was distracting, but it seems I did not hinder your performance any."

Peggy quickly bobbed another curtsy. She was obviously impressed that one of the classed passengers would condescend to make her acquaintance.

Hannah almost let the impression persist. It felt nice to be considered privileged. In all reality, she was indeed fortunate to avoid travelling steerage. But there was honesty in her that refused to let it pass. "I cannot stay long – the obligations of my service duties call me. But it was lovely to meet you, Peggy." Hannah turned her head to indicate where Lady Whitmore was chatting and caught the eye of a man standing not far away, considering their conversation with a frown. "That man over there... he seems unhappy that we are talking. Is he your husband?"

"Who? Husband? Oh no, I'm fourteen! That is only George, my brother. He gets concerned that I like to think above my station... and age."

"Well, be reassured, as I mentioned, I have no station to speak of. And I appreciate friends of any age. I did just want to say that I enjoyed watching your skill with the rope. Perhaps we can talk more?"

Peggy's eyes lit up. "That would be lovely, Ma'am."

"Hannah. Just Hannah."

"Yes, Hannah Ma'am."

Hannah smiled and said she would try and meet her on the morrow.

18.

They sat together in the dining galley. The sea was calm, and the ship had stalled in the quiet absence of wind. It was eerie, the way the sails hung limp, and the sound of the waves slapping against the hull was stilled.

Hannah was playing the piano, accompanying someone who was giving an ordinary rendition of a dreary ballad. As they finished, there was a bored smattering of light applause. Lady Whitmore sat there sipping her drink. "I think I prefer the roll of the waves. The singing is appalling, and the silence of the sea is entirely too uncanny for my comfort."

"It feels strange for sure," offered Hannah uneasily as she sat back down. "Everyone is talking about the calm before a storm. Do you think we are headed for a squall?"

Sebastian raised his glass. "We are not headed anywhere in this dead calm. The captain has not mentioned anything about a storm, so I am going to enjoy the lack of motion." And he poured another drink.

Lady Whitmore looked at him, took a sip of her drink and cleared her throat. "Hannah dear, could you give me a moment with Sebastian? We need some time and the confines of the ship hardly allow it."

Hannah quickly stood to her feet. "Yes, M'Lady, of course. I will continue collating the files, if Mr Digby is happy for me to do that unsupervised."

Sebastian waved his glass. "Greif, Hannah, when have I worried about supervising you? Do whatever amuses you. I thought perhaps you may prefer to read."

"It would a relief to have that task completed. It seems to have gone on too long."

He shrugged and took another drink. Hannah frowned and left for his cabin to continue transferring onto a ledger the tied bundles of documents now stacked in the trunk. Aunty Biddy turned to him. "Sebastian? What is going on?"

"Very little I would say, Aunt Biddy. Seems a sailboat cannot sail without a breeze. Not going anywhere…"

"Sebastian. Listen to me. Your father has made a fuss your entire life about your capabilities… or lack of them. After you left university, what did you do?"

"Nothing at all, as I recall. He said that often enough. As did you. Regardless of what my professors wanted, being a scholar of law didn't fit well. Or I didn't fit it. Aside from the church, or the military, it seems law is the only option presented if you are landed gentry without land."

"Pish-posh and twaddle. This is not about career choices; nor that you never sat in chambers. Whatever your father determined was your lot, you were unyielding in your pursuit to be the exact opposite. When you turned down the jobs he sourced, he declared you would end up a miserable outcast. And yet you became the most invited, sought after, social creature who had everyone tripping over themselves to have you part of their circle. You were everything he said you could not be."

He nodded with a smirk. It was not often he was allowed to believe that he had out manoeuvred his father.

Aunt Biddy put down her drink. "So, my question is this: how did you do that?"

He shrugged. "Ate cheese and drank wine. It is the nourishment of the elite."

"And… ?"

"Okay. I disguised myself in fashion... and took dancing lessons. Studied stories. Chummied up to the social butterflies and became their own little chrysalis. Gave them the pleasure of seeing me emerge to fly around their handsome gardens."

"Exactly! Research. You learnt what was needed to fit that life and you did it. I remember you scraping together for a particular cravat... just because it was stylish. It cost you. But you excelled."

"Aunt Biddy, I'm pretty sure a well-executed quadrille or a fancy cummerbund is not going to make any difference here."

"Humph! I doubt any barbarian who calls Australia home would have the slightest notion what a quadrille even is. Not my point. The point is – you proved him wrong. You studied your goal and resourced yourself to accomplish exactly what he didn't expect."

"And...?"

"Don't be dull, Sebastian. Do the same here. He thinks you can't make a life for yourself in the colony. He thinks you can't manage property, or workers, or acclimatise socially and politically. He thinks he has already won, and you have already lost. But he doesn't know you at all. However, I do. And I know you are proud and capable, and definitely not stupid."

"Am I to be reassured knowing that you have twigged to the real me? You've always known me, Aunt Biddy. This is not new. Hannah on the other hand..."

"First things first, Sebastian. You need to take some dancing lessons and buy yourself a fashionable cravat... or whatever the Australian equivalent of that is. Sebastian, do the research and prove that repulsive shadow of a man who was supposed to be your father, that he is wrong."

Sebastian took another drink. "What if I can't do this?"

"Hannah says you underestimate yourself. There has never been a more sensible assessment of a situation.'"

"Hannah says she is undecided. What is undecided is whether I can actually do it at all." Was he capable of being a farmer in an unknown land? He shrugged. His sensible assessment was that he genuinely didn't know.

"To my mind a better question to ask is, 'What do I need to do this? I truly believe Hannah has no idea just how much she has underestimated the underestimated."

Sebastian took another drink... and another... and he almost said it. He almost asked her about the letter and the rumour that he knew full well had been embraced as gospel-truth by his miserable family. And he despaired on how to dig for the actual truth of who he really was. The more appalling horror would be that this unknowing would go on forever. The truth was buried so deep it could never come to light. The only glimmer of light was that Hannah knew this secret disgrace and she had not turned away... not completely. There was still a sliver of hope.

Hannah worked for a while on the ledger. But the frustration of the task and the stuffy stillness of the cabin drove her outside for some fresh air. How could Sebastian ever see his way through this? She really wanted to do something that would make a difference. She wanted to give him a push, like a toddler learning to walk, so that he would get up and run like the athlete she believed him to be.

She hovered near the lights by the main door that spluttered with cheap whale blubber. The deck was still and smoky and a number of couples were walking around the deck. Hannah knew the darkness on these nights fed the superstitions of sailors. She craned her neck hoping for the slightest puff of a breeze. "Oh, Miss Johnson. Good evening." George snatched his hat from his head, kneading it in his hands.

"Mr Toms. Good evening. It is very still. I was hoping for the relief of some fresh sea air."

He shook his head at her. "I'm thinking sea air that stinks of fish-barrels and briny water is never going to be fresh. Still... it is a fair change from sleeping in that undercarriage of hell. Wasn't born a rabbit to live underground and below deck is an equal affliction. I could never have been a miner."

She had spoken to George a couple of times after Peggy introduced them. He always wore that glaring frown she first noticed after the deck games. This was different. She had not expected Peggy's brother to have an affable side. "Well, it seems we both seek the same thing: some respite from inside."

"It is good we have bumped into each other. I have been wanting to speak to you since Peggy told me of your acquaintance with... your travel companions." George swept his hat forward as an invitation to walk and Hannah fell in step with him along the deck.

Hannah raised her brow. "Really on what topic? We have so little in common."

"Well, I could say it is an opportunity to learn each other's interests… but I have a much more practical purpose. Peggy and I have no position in Australia. We got notice just before we boarded that the appointment, we had hoped for fell through because an unfortunate situation has taken our sponsors. We didn't declare those details because it would have risked our passage. Peggy asked me to talk to you. We are hoping to secure some new contacts before we arrive. She wondered if you knew of anyone looking to hire. With the people you meet, you might know someone needing a farmhand and milkmaid. Peggy is very good at domestic duties and more than a fair cook."

"You're looking for a position? I hardly think I am the …" and Hannah stopped mid-sentence. "Although… perhaps I can assist. My Lady and her Godson are seeking support in their new venture. Perhaps such practical experience is exactly what they need. What sort of farming do you do?"

"Cropping and shepherding mostly. Done a bit with cattle… mainly dairy. Know horses. And poultry. I think I am what the colony calls a general hand and all-round roustabout."

Suddenly Hannah felt very optimistic. George Toms' broad experience qualified him for an unknown farm in an unknown land. They turned about again, and they walked away from the lamps further into the shadows. She didn't see Sebastian at the door with a shocked look of jealous rage flickering in the lamplight. When she and George made the next turn, he had already disappeared down the galley stairs.

Sebastian slammed the door to his cabin. He furiously swept the untied pile of documents off his desk and sent them flying over the floor like tickertape, and hunkered down, pummelling his pillow, and tried to numb his disgust in sleep.

19

This steerage dance was the talk of the ship. The storm never came, but neither did the winds. It was an uncanny problem that had the captain, first-mate and crew debating at length about this unseasonal lull, all the while having no solutions to puff out the sails. Distraction became their strategy.

"So, Miss Hannah, introduce me to your friend." Sebastian spoke above the fiddler's tunes reminiscent of an English public house.

"Well. Okay. This is Miss Toms: Miss Penelope Toms. Peggy, this is Mr Digby."

"Oh, Peggy of the rope-skipping fame? Really?" His grin showed he was a little amused.

"Yes Sir." Peggy bobbed a curtsy.

"Penelope? Well, that is a fine name. A little surprising though," he said with a heavy dose of charm.

Peggy looked confused, and stuttered a little, unsure what was expected of her. Was it not enough that a fine gentleman had taken note of her jump-rope accomplishments?

"Are you not curious why I think so?"

"Yes, Sir. If you want me to be."

"Penelope is a name for ladies of nobility. I am surprised that you would be a rope-skipping champion. Quite undignified."

"Oh Sir, do you think so? I am sorry to embarrass you, Sir."

Hannah spoke above the noise. "Peggy, it is fine. If you want to jump rope, you can. Mr Digby does his own share of activities to embarrass himself." She glared at Sebastian. Was this scrutiny of names his only lead-in to flirt with the ladies? She felt cheapened that this very same conversation, in a ballroom, not so far in the past, had captured her attention.

"But I would never mean to…" stammered Peggy.

Sebastian nodded with a bow. "Miss Penelope. Perhaps I have a solution to all the embarrassment. Partner me for the Strip-the-Willow and all will be forgiven."

"Oh, but I couldn't."

"No? Why not?"

"My brother prefers that I only dance with him."

"Oh. Well, that is a little awkward, when he is quite at liberty to partner whomever he likes. Isn't that so, Miss Hannah? Why do you think there would be such sibling discrepancy?"

"Sorry, Sir? I don't understand," stammered Peggy again.

"Why can your brother dance and keep company with whomever he pleases; and you are only allowed to dance with him?"

"Well, he is being protective, Sir."

"Mr Digby! Can I speak with you? Please!" said Hannah firmly. "Alone!"

Sebastian nodded a bow in Peggy's direction and retreated to the side with his hands behind his back. He turned to Hannah. "*Alone* seems to be your forté."

"Since we are speaking of alone: leave Peggy *alone*. She is quite confused by your banter. Although she is tall, she is very young, just fourteen. It is appropriate that her brother is protective. She does not understand you or the way you tease."

"And yet you do? I don't think you understand me at all, Miss Hannah."

"So, you keep asserting. But I know that you have no concern for Peggy aside from the amusement of a jolly dance.   I don't want her heart broken because some handsome man with a cabin-pass, tips his hat in her direction. Once again, I insist that you leave her alone."

"Your concern for her is very touching. You want me to let her alone, yet you don't want anything to do with me either. Are you out to isolate me from the comfort of any companionship?"

"Oh please. You are being dramatic, Sebastian. This is just a respectful request, one friend to another."

"Friend? Pttf!'

"You doubt that?"

"A friend would not behave the way you do. A friend would *never* meet Farmer George to go walking alone! You are my aunt's companion. She doesn't need the gossip or the indignity."

"What are you talking about? I only talk to Mr Toms with his sister present."

"Hannah your pretence of being cloistered is sickening.   You have shown yourself to be blatantly shameless."

"What are you talking about?" she repeated.

"I'm talking about moon-lit deck walks... with the Farmer."

"Is this why you have been avoiding me? Is this why you suddenly turn up your nose at my company and will not let me help with the documents? You think I have been visiting with George Toms behind your back, meeting him in secret because we are admirers? That is preposterous!"

"Preposterous would be a relief. This is disgusting."

"You accuse myself of dubious standards, and yet you had me help in your cabin alone without pause. Think about who is calling the kettle black, Mr Digby."

"I thought your show of reluctance was nothing other than modest propriety. I now know why you returned the ring. Your pretty speech means nothing. I had no idea how wrong I was!"

"Not that wrong at all, it seems, if that is what you think. Good day, Mr Digby. Good day!" Hannah turned on her heel and left the deck. She went straight to Lady Whitmore's cabin and sat silently on a chair and picked up a book. But the words sat on the page unwilling to tell their story. In the end she put down the book and picked up her handiwork piece. She pricked her finger with the needle in her agitation and flung it aside. Then she took up a drawing sheet and charcoal. She put that down and returned to her book. She smudged the page with the black char on her fingers, and a smear of blood. She put that down, got up and wiped her hands on a towel staring out the small porthole like a caged bird. In the end the confines of the cabin drove her outside once more. She intended to go to the dining room, but she passed some passengers in the galley who nodded an acknowledgment and mentioned Lady Whitmore was inside. The thought of her penetrating questions was entirely too disconcerting. She was drawn back to the fringes of the steerage dance staying close to the shadows, watching the dancers galloping to the jaunty tunes.

"Here you are. I was looking for you. Peggy said you left suddenly."

She jolted. Sebastian's accusation rang loud in her ears. "Oh. Mr Toms. I promise I will speak with my employer tomorrow. I should be able to give you a response by the end of the week. I do not wish to encourage optimism though. It seems I may have spoken too quickly out of a misplaced understanding. I am sorry if I have given you false hope. There may not be a job for you and your sister after all."

"No matter. I am grateful you considered sponsoring a good word for us."

"To no end it would seem. My sincerest apologies, Mr Toms." She turned to go.

"Miss Hannah? Why all the formality? Did we not see eye to eye? If I don't get a job there, I will somewhere else. They say jobs are going begging for people who know farming." He held his hat in his hands, massaging it in a way that was obliterating its shape. "Perhaps you would consider getting hitched, as my wife?"

She froze. "I'm sorry, what?" Was Sebastian suddenly a prophet?

"Get married: you and me. I work hard. I can support both you and Peggy."

"I cannot marry you, Mr Toms. I am spoken for."

"You are? Oh? I thought since you no longer..." He looked at her hand and stared at her empty fingers with a frown.

"Oh well... the ring... there was a problem with the sizing. None the less, it is not possible. But I am flattered at the invitation and the regard that it shows."

"Hmm. Well, if you change your mind..."

"If I change my mind, I will let you know, Mr Toms. To be sure." She closed her eyes and turned away. She heard his feet shuffle and then fade as he left. The music transitioned to a jig, and she watched partners form and join hands. She noticed with some relief that George had already secured a partner. His heart was evidently not shattered by her refusal. She held onto a pole. She suddenly felt unstable even though the deck remained motionless in the stagnant sea. She closed her eyes and saw in her mind the laughing smile of Sebastian rolling with the music, tapping out polka dance steps. It seemed that they instinctively knew how to keep time with each other: their dances, their games, their banter. This discord between them was jarring. The timing was out, and it felt unnatural. But she didn't know what to do about it.

Hannah yawned and thought perhaps she had calmed enough to settle for the night. She turned to make her way back to the cabin and jolted. Sebastian was standing right there behind her.

"Miss Hannah? May I keep company for a moment, since you are here unaccompanied? It hardly seems appropriate to have two individuals alone while the rest of the ship dances the evening away."

"Mr Digby, you need not bother yourself to be so benevolent towards my plight. Considering the shame, I inflict on your aunt's reputation; you risk being tainted by association. I have stood in dance halls before without partners, suffering no sense of unease. This is no exception."

"See, Miss Hannah, I think you are entirely right. You do know how to be alone so elegantly."

"You make it sound like I am some sort of sole comet tracking across the sky."

"And if you were, your unique celestial beauty is only highlighted by the velvet night."

"No need for flattery, Mr Digby. I can survive without it."

"Perhaps. But me? I feel lost in this cosmos."

"Sebastian how can you go from accusing me of being a morally loose little trollop, to pleading with me to keep you company? It is beyond reason."

"I didn't say you were a tramp."

"Of course, you did. You accused me of soliciting the affections of another. If that is what happened – it was unconsciously done, without the scheming and the plotting you suggest."

"Oh, come on, Hannah! How can I stand silently by while other men are fawning all over you for attention?"

"There are a few things I find quite perverse with that claim. One: that you accuse me of being the cause of your problem. Two: you insist that you are rendered powerless. And Thirdly: why would you doubt our friendship? Can you not trust me to be faithful in our friendship? Regardless of whether there is courtship involved."

"See: friendship. It is exactly as you say. You are the daughter of a Rector. Even he would suggest that the Almighty knows that it is not good to be alone. We need a helpmeet along the way. You are my helpmeet – Hannah of the maids-and-cooks. So, meet me… help me!"

"Hmm… that sounds so entirely despairing and abandoned. Helping is one thing; but this? This desperation sounds so completely unattractive and appalling to me."

"So, the list gets longer?"

"I am not afraid of hard work, Sebastian. I do want to help you in what we are going to, but don't refuse to take responsibility for your part. You are above that."

"Is it possible, Hannah of the 'maids-and-cooks', that I will never satisfy your insatiable need to prove you are better than me?"

"You say that because I am not intimidated by you, regardless of your title, and my lack of station! I swear you are the most unacknowledged combination of capacity and ability in a man I know. And the thing is – it is not me who doesn't recognise this. Give yourself more recognition, Sebastian!"

"What? No slights about illegitimacy, or immoral roots. No dig about unredeemed debts? Even I know that if you told these superstitious sailors of my true position, they would throw me overboard to counteract the weather and bring back the wind."

She shook her head. "Do you really think you are at the mercy of random superstitions? God is in control of our destiny, Sebastian, but we still have to put our hand to the plough. I want us to get through this, Sebastian, but I wonder if you do. It seems you always have something else to blame."

He looked out over the still, inky ocean. "Hannah, why would you meet Farmer George on the deck in the dark? It is entirely insulting that you prefer his company to mine."

"Oh Please! I did not *arrange* to meet him. It was per chance. But I put that chance to good use. You think I do everything for selfish reasons, but I do want to help. I really do."

"By throwing yourself at his feet?"

"I can't just wait on my laurels while you expect the help we need to fall from the sky. He asked for a reference for a job on your farm. He was telling me a list of his experiences. I was going to speak to you and Lady Whitmore about it tomorrow. He is interested in working for you."

"I bet he is. You want him to work for me so you can see him more frequently. Why would I do that? So, you can marry *him*?"

"Sebastian, let me help you with that little foray into fantasy! I won't marry him. He already asked. I said no. He is not a romantic interest. And you are fast *not* becoming one either. This spoilt boy act of yours is very tiresome!"

20.

Aunt Biddy sat on the buggy with the forbearance of a saint. The term 'Buggy' actually suggested a level of comfort, but the only vehicle they could secure was more like a farm cart fitted with planks. The distances of nothingness between settlements defied logic. Biddy didn't complain but her face was taut, her forehead furrowed. The signs of a headache were starting to show, evidenced as she closed her eyes against the light with the cover of her shawl; she groaned and held her head when the horses jarred, or a wheel hit a rut. In a moment of weakness, she leaned hard against Hannah while Peggy tried to soften the jolting by adding cushions around the hard seat. "Don't fuss child! It will not make the trip go quicker. Surely, we will stop soon." Peggy retreated under her rebuke.

"I understand there is a way-side inn coming up, but not for a while yet," offered Hannah.

"This is intolerable. Send me back to the ship! Even when we were rounding The Cape in mountainous seas, that pitiful raft was better than this. What I would not give to just lie down?"

"Yes, M'Lady. That would be entirely more consoling."

"Don't patronise me, Hannah. I am doing the best that I can."

"We all are, M'Lady. You are doing well in unreasonable circumstances."

"Where is Sebastian?"

"He rode ahead, Lady Whitmore. He said he would secure us rooms."

"Humph. Distract me. Tell me again why you two could not get along?"

"M'Lady, it is not my place. Sebastian has his reasons."

"And you have yours. You don't have to divulge all the details of his callous and unfeeling heart, just enough to divert me from this infernal journey. But if you could stand it, a little embellishment may help."

"Oh M'Lady, I am not good at telling stories like Sebastian. You will not be entertained by my account."

"I don't need to be entertained. Only distracted. What is it? Is he not handsome enough?"

"But of course, he is good looking."

"*Handsome*. You can say it. He has a manner about him like my Eddie. Handsome to the core. And he knew it too. Used it to charm his way around all sorts of problems."

"M'Lady! I am shocked that you would consider this important."

"Oh pish-posh and twaddle, Hannah. Can't hurt to enjoy what we wake up next to."

"Well, I am pretty sure I would appreciate any man whom I loved enough to wake up with."

Peggy blushed at their candid talk and bustled to the front seat of the cart and sat with her brother. She stared at the little dust willy-willies swirling away like spinning tops across the ground. Everything was yellow, crunchy, and dry; so different to the lush farmlands where she came from. Peggy looked out over the hills, rolling on and on, into miles of nothing. To her it was the most exhilarating depiction of expansiveness she had ever experienced.

"M'Lady, the thing is that Sebastian never did say... well, he *won't* say that he loves me. He only concedes that I make him wild with jealousy, or that he needs me on this endeavour, so it makes sense to him. For someone who is so articulate and expressive in every other matter, I thought that if he truly loved me, he would simply declare it."

"Love is not a simple matter."

"But I am not inclined to marry because I am the cause of crazed episodes of insanity or for my abilities of practical insight. He asked me once what my non-negotiable would be in a marriage and I told him that I would marry for love. That is probably the only impractical thing that I have ever permitted myself. And perhaps I will miss out altogether, but it is something that I have resolved to allow. Were you and Lord Edward in love, Lady Whitmore?"

"Infatuated in the most scandalous way. And I never regretted it. This Australian voyage would have been such an adventure for Eddie. I try to remember that when the going is rough. It is what I thought about while that ship was driving through that vicious storm, waves the size of mountains, praying I would die. Every day adds depth to our story, and if it means one of those days takes me out, it is not to be regretted because I was wading through life, all in... fully immersed in every experience. Eddie taught me that."

"Oh M'Lady, *that* is what I saw in Sebastian. But it seemed he lost it at some point." She paused. She knew exactly when it was lost. "I thought he would embrace this adventure. But he doesn't want this quest. It seems he wants someone to blame if it doesn't work out. That was why. Yes, that is why we came to odds. I wouldn't let him put that on me." She lowered her voice and leant in close. "Well… that, and the fact he accused me of shaming you with the most debaucherous and illicit behaviour. I was very angry at him for that."

"Ahh. Hence the proviso that Mr Toms was not to tilt his farmer's hat in your direction."

"He told you I was flirting with Mr Toms?" she whispered behind her hand.

"I think he described it as throwing yourself at his feet."

"Oh, Lady Whitmore, tell me you did not believe him! Why ever would you allow Sebastian to sign Mr Toms on under such circumstances?"

"Oh pish-posh. One conversation with that man and I could tell Mr Toms has not the right colour of hair or temperament for you. Solid? Hard worker? Of course. Protective of his family? Definitely. All good qualities. And even if you did change your mind on Mr Toms, no one would blame you – you could do a lot worse. Lord Sideburns for example."

Hannah relaxed and smiled from relief. "We could enjoy a pleasant game of whist while we travel. It would be a diverting way to pass the time," she said with a sophisticated lilt brushing away the flies.

"Greif! Can you imagine? Hannah, do you know how I know?"

Hannah shrugged and took the canvas water bag that hung on the side of the buggy to pour a drink into a cup. The cart lurched and some of it spilled on her pinafore. Lady

Whitmore took it and proceeded with her observations. "When you are with Sebastian it is like you come alive. You both do. Whether it is from frustration or fun, it doesn't seem to matter. That is the difference between Sebastian and Farmer Toms or Lord Sideburns. He is your 'tell', and I suggest you don't undertake to learn poker any time soon, because you would give yourself away and lose to the point of complete destitution."

"M'Lady! I am a Rector's daughter. That you would suggest…"

"No matter. Sebastian has his own tells. He drives himself around a mountain a dozen times, but he always comes back to the same driveway. He always came back to Whytehaven Hall. That was his home, no matter how many other places tried to claim him as their own. You are his Whytehaven now, Hannah. I believe that. He will come back to you."

21.

When they pulled up outside the hotel, Hannah took Lady Whitmore straight to their room. It was dingy and basic and the cabin on the ship seemed entirely luxurious in comparison. The thing about exhaustion is that it reduces the dilemma of less than clean linen because lying down becomes the supreme luxury. Hannah drew the dusty curtains. Lady Whitmore closed her ears to the ruckus from the pub downstairs and was asleep in seconds. Sebastian had booked the last room available, so they dragged two additional mattresses into the room for Peggy and herself.

Hannah slowly walked back down the stairs into the rowdy, smoky dining room for something to eat. Every table was taken, so there was no hope for a quiet corner to eat her meal. Perhaps camping under starlight had its advantages. She found Peggy and Mr Toms eating stew; she put down her bowl and pulled across an empty chair to sit with them. Peggy looked distressed. "Miss, we are not to eat with you. We do not want to lose our jobs."

"That's ridiculous. I'm not going to sit with people I don't know. I feel safer with you than anyone else in this room."

"But Mr Digby said…"

"Mr Digby is not here, and he cannot keep me from talking with friends."

George looked significantly to the corner where a jaunty tune was being bashed out on the out-of-tune upright piano. Hannah turned around and followed the direction of his nod. Sebastian was there, with a very buxom woman sitting on his knee. She was giggling at the comments he whispered in her ear... and with horror she saw his hand wander unapologetically up over her thighs. Hannah almost dropped her spoon as she gagged on her mouthful. She quickly took a gulp from the glass on the table, without realising she had helped herself to Peggy's drink. She stood up, shaking. The girl giggled flirtatiously, and Sebastian's eyes flashed as they connected with Hannah's gaze across the room. He deliberately leant in, whispering in her ear as his hand stroked her thigh. Then still holding Hannah's stare he took another swig of his ale. Hannah slammed down the mug and left the room, going straight up to their quarters. It was cramped, grimy and smelly, and she didn't care. Nothing could feel as contaminated as what she had just witnessed.

⁕⁕⁕⁕⁕⁕

Hannah completed her ablutions and returned from the long drop out the back. She made her way via the kitchen to collect a breakfast tray for Lady Whitmore. She knocked before she entered. "Are you ready, M'Lady? I have breakfast for you." She opened the door to find Lady Whitmore still in bed, her bedcap firmly in place. "M'Lady today is the last leg of the trip. Tonight, we will all be sleeping in our own beds."

"Hannah dear. I can't. I am unwell. So unwell. If yesterday was intolerable, today I feel like I have been pummelled-by-a-thousand-stampeding-camels.   I really cannot go anywhere. Not today."

Hannah looked at her puffy eyes, pasty colour and believed that she was in no way exaggerating. Lady

134

Whitmore was not one to loiter in a bed all day; especially a bed like this.

"Okay… well… I'll find Mr Digby and find out what he wants to do. Here is some bread and tea, M'Lady, on your tray. See if you can eat."

"Humph. Can't eat. Might try the tea."

"Be warned, M'Lady. It is in line with the scrapings of a peat-bog… like on the ship." Hannah paled and shook her head. Sebastian invaded life at every turn; every turn of phrase. She felt unsteady. She had not slept well either. Her eyes were red and her skin blotchy. How could she do this? Just focus. Focus on Lady Whitmore.

"Hannah, you are not falling victim to this illness too, are you?"

"No, M'Lady. I am fine." She asserted it again to herself with emphasis. *Just fine!* Sebastian – Mr Digby, had made it perfectly clear. All his talk of marriage, but that was not what he intended at all. No, right now she needed to focus on Lady Whitmore. Lady Whitmore alone. She walked to the door and tried to think how she could locate him after such a night. She would not go trowelling through guest rooms hoping to fall upon the particular parlour to which he had been invited into. She decided to go out to the stable. George Toms was harnessing the horses with Baker, a young stable-hand who had been hired to join their endeavour. "Good morning, Toms, have you seen Mr Digby this morning?"

He looked at her with sympathy. "Hmm. I have. Out by the wagon."

"Okay." She took a breath and strode frostily over to the wagon where he was securing their luggage. "Oh, you are up, Mr Digby. I thought you might be still..." She took another deep breath. *No. Leave it alone. I am just here for Lady Whitmore*, she reminded herself.

Sebastian looked at her and jumped down to her side. "Good morning! Today our lives are forever changed, and we see what all this carry-on has been about. Is Aunt Biddy ready?"

Seriously? Would he not even feel the slightest twinge of remorse? But no, he seemed like himself. More like himself than he had been for a long time actually. "This is what I need to talk to you about. Lady Whitmore is sick. She will not be able to travel today. I wanted to check what you wanted to do. Will I stay with her?"

"Here? This is entirely not a suitable place to convalesce."

"It was a suitable lay-over last night," she said bitterly. "Besides, there is nowhere else. She really cannot travel, Mr Digby."

"Well okay. Give me a minute to think." He walked around the wagon and checked the secured ropes. By the time he had done a circuit of the rope anchors, he stopped and lent against the load. "I will see Eliza and determine if a bigger room has become available for Aunt Biddy. Peggy will stay with her on a trundle bed. Toms can take the wagon. Baker can ride and lead the horses. You and me in the buggy. We will come back and to fetch her home once she has had a chance to rest."

"I am going with you? Shouldn't I be staying with her?"

"Probably, and if there is a way you can duplicate yourself, Hannah so you can be in two places, I would be happy to hear it."

"But..."

"I need you to sort out the house, so that when Aunt Biddy arrives, she will be comfortable. I'll organise the room straight away so you can move her things. Make sure Peggy cleans the room thoroughly every day. I want to leave as soon as she is settled, so we are not too late at the other end." He strode towards the hotel, and Hannah was left staring after him.

They shuffled the things into Aunt Biddy's travel portmanteaux and moved her to a twin room with an adjoining doorway. Sebastian said it was the best Eliza had to offer. Hannah was quiet and did not say much except to relay Digby's instructions. "I'm sorry, Lady Whitmore that I cannot stay with you. Please let Peggy look after you. We will be back within the week to fetch you home." Lady Whitmore waved her hand weakly; too sick to object even if the plan was not to her liking.

Sebastian came and said goodbye. As he left, he turned to Peggy. "If you need anything, talk to Eliza – she is in charge of the housekeeping and maids. She has assured me that no one will bother you. If they do, make sure Eliza knows." He jumped up into the buggy and before he flicked the reigns, he turned to Hannah sitting stiffly on the seat beside him. "So, Hannah. Are you ready to see what adventure awaits us in this new chapter called 'Australian farming life'?"

Hannah wanted to stay indifferent and detached. She turned to him and searched his eyes, and he returned her gaze, clear and smiling. Perhaps there were a few things resolved for him. Perhaps he was now as devoted to this Eliza, as he had once indicated he was to her. She shook her head confused. "No, not as ready as I had hoped," she admitted.

He laughed. "Well. Let's go and see what awaits us."

22.

With unbending resolution, Hannah refused to pretend everything was okay. She was going out to the property in the manner of an ambassador posted to some foreign embassy. It was a metaphor that appealed to her, even if it edged over the sensible line into fanciful. It was more palatable than thinking of Sebastian as the enemy. This way she could negotiate diplomatically to represent her homeland's wishes, working together on formal and remote terms. But courtship? Impossible! Even friendship was off the table. The buggy hit a rut and she reached out to steady herself. Sebastian noted that she clung to the side of the seat with her face turned away.

With a careful tone he questioned her. "Are you okay? Obviously, the progress of the British Empire has not taken responsibility for their network of thoroughfares. Her Majesty would do well to learn from the Romans. Their roads still stand."

"Perhaps the British contingent of convicts does not extend to the all-embracing resources that Julius Caesar had access to," she said stiffly.

"Or maybe this is as good as a convict highway gets. Perhaps we really are beyond the backend of nowhere, and we are now officially passed the realms of known civilisation."

An old man kangaroo bounded across the track, and the horses barely missed a step. "Oh my! Did you see how huge that kangaroo was!" she exclaimed in amazement. She couldn't get used to this strange country.

Sebastian raised his brow and said, "That's one."

"No! That is not what I meant. I am not playing *Feathered and Furred*. Definitely not! I was just observing it is the most peculiar animal. It is bizarre how they stand on two legs and jump around."

"Your detachment does not mean I cannot play. I have done so on many solo excursions to amuse myself. But be warned, I am not a quiet player unless there is a reward in play. Feathered! Well, this is an unexpected challenge. I have already seen four different types of enormous parrots! Black like a raven but with red splashes across their tail; white with a brilliant yellow crest; grey and pink; green and red. I've even heard they do the impossible here and have *black* swans. Can you imagine?" Sebastian travelled his eyes over the scrub around them. It was the strangest place, again stepping through the covers of a child's reader into a world of imagination. Nothing seemed like it could be intentional – the uncomfortable colour pallet, the bizarre animals and strange birds. Trees with long, narrow leaves, like the fletching feathers on an arrow shaft. A laugh of a kookaburra rang out, mocking them as other birds screeched and squawked in an agony of bush torture. The white tipped ginger tail of a dog flicked as it eyed them skittishly from the underbrush. Sebastian leaned over and pointed to a large bird, obviously not an ostrich, plainer in its colour. A flock of some sort of pigeon, strange in its markings, scrawnier in its size was disturbed and flew up over the horses and they threw back their manes.

Hannah shook her head. "All this strangeness is a bit overwhelming."

Sebastian was drawn in by its fascinating magnetic pull. It defied his experience, but somehow it felt more real and unpretentious than the soft greens of the genteel English countryside. He pointed, "Bizarre animal number three. Unknown bird number six."

"I've lost complete confidence that I am actually seeing what I am seeing," said Hannah as she was enticed into sharing his observations. "What exactly is that?"

"The beak is like a raven in the style and fame of the Tower of London, but it is pied, and listen… its song is quite pleasant! Remarkable."

Hannah stared around her wide-eyed. "Even the flowers are strange. They are not pretty like an English rose. So unusual.   That looks like my grandmother's feather-duster."

Sebastian smiled and felt slightly smug she had not stayed aloof. Once again, he was on the dance floor, cajoling her to keep time. "I believe we need another category: Feathered, Furred and *Flower*. Excellent development. Flowers are now part of the rules."

"But there are so few. Perhaps it is the wrong time of year."

"All the more intriguing if you can spot a bloom. How about that one? It looks like a fire lantern sitting up like that. Completely odd."

"I had no idea this would be so… unexpected," said Hannah.

"This has certainly taken 'unusual' further than I imagined. Welcome to Australia Hannah," said Sebastian softly. "Is this enough adventure for you?"

❦

23.

They pulled up outside the homestead. Hannah placed her gloved hand over her mouth in horror. The place was deserted and broken down; the harsh Australian weather had prematurely aged the buildings which in English terms were still brand new. Sebastian jumped down and helped Hannah on the step. "Come. Let's do the tour so we can at least unload the beds."

They walked through the gate. The caretakers that Roderick had installed in his absence had not done a good job. A scruffy beard appeared on the verandah step sporting a long-barrelled musket. He scanned the wagon, buggy, and horses. "Who are ye and what do ye want?" he growled in a thick Irish accent, pointing the barrel at them.

Sebastian stopped and pushed Hannah behind him. He eyed the ancient firearm and the grim line of the man's mouth as he chewed his way around some tobacco. He spat and splattered a rank smear down the post and over the rail. The dark stains on the timber indicated this was not the first time he had done that. He walked down the stairs, automatically stepping over a broken plank. Sebastian and Hannah backed out through the gateway; the gate hanging limp on its hinge. Perhaps there never had been a caretaker appointed. Perhaps Roderick had sold it in a back-handed deal, and there was no bequest to claim at all. Sebastian sighed. It would be ironic if he had to put his legal studies to work now after all the dodging he had done to avoid working at law. "We came to introduce ourselves to the landowner here. We are the new neighbours, and just on our way through. This your place? Or is the owner around?" Sebastian asked, respectfully cautious.

The man straightened up and squared his shoulders. "My spread. I's the boss 'ere," he said in a thick Irish brogue.

Okay… so not the caretaker. "Well so very delighted to make your acquaintance," said Sebastian, hale and hearty, and he leaned in to give a handshake. "Glad to have met our neighbours."

The man jolted to attention and poked the loaded musket in his chest. "Not so fast, Mister. I ain't heard of any new neighbours."

Sebastian paused, and then dropped his arm in despair. "Really? Well, that *is* embarrassing! I tried to make all the noise I could about coming here. I paid such an excellent price for that there spread. Was hoping it might drive values up if people around could hear how land is so eagerly sought after. That would be to all our advantage." Sebastian took off his hat and ran his hand through his hair, and sighed. "You really heard nothing? Damn! Nothing at all?"

"Oh… well. I do kinda keep to myself."

"Well, I thought… you know… given times being so tough and all."

Sebastian kept Toms in his peripheral vision, coming in from around the back. The man lowered his gun and nodded sagely. "Right you are," O'Grady said. "Tough."

"So, this is a nice-looking place. How long have you been here?"

"Seven years. Moved in when the last guy just walked off. Left it wide open. Here I am."

"Really? As easy as that? Wish someone had told me that was a possibility. I might have done the deal next door differently had I known that was a way," he said with a mischievous grin.

The man smirked with him. Suddenly he was the clever one in this conversation. "Yep. All I got to do is stay on for twelve years and the spread is mine. All legal. And so, I haven't left. Not once. Five to go. The toff that was here, just up and left. People kept coming around looking for what is their due, but I'd just peg at them until they left. But haven't heard hide nor hair of him or where he went. Rumoured he skedaddled back to the Mother Country." He sniggered, and then a light dawned in his eyes as he felt a pistol barrel jam under his ribs as George came up behind him.

Sebastian calmly reached out and took his musket. "Consider your tenancy terminated. That toff was my brother who sent us *from* the Mother Country to take his place. So, I actually have the official title deed. My place. My spread."

"What about the neighbours," he stammered.

Sebastian smirked. "We have neighbours? Well, that sounds entirely social. We will be sure to look them up." He eyed him up and down.

O'Grady swore. "Should've let them torch the whole damn place. They tried you know. I put the fires out me-self. Only lost the meat-house."

"Seems to me that generous act of charity means you had somewhere to stay… and now you owe me seven years rent. You can work it off, day for day… or you can leave and never show your face around here again. I will consider that to be *my* benevolent gesture for not literally taking my pound of flesh out of your despicable, bony frame. What is it going to be?"

He glared and let loose with a volley of expletives as Toms restrained him from behind.

"Excellent choice, sir," Sebastian said happily. "Straight away would be an entirely appropriate time frame. Take one horse. Everything else stays." The man narrowed his eyes sullenly, his face glowering resentfully. But Sebastian was not finished. "Baker, go and see what horses are here. Cull the worst. He can have that."

The man thrashed in a frustrated rage. He lashed out like a crazy cut snake, raring up he kicked Sebastian under the ribs. The musket flew from his hands and blasted loudly as it hit the ground. Toms big frame quickly pinned him down again. Sebastian doubled over, gasping for breath. "Oh please! Am I going to have to take you in and add assault to your sheet? Or will you just go?" The inconvenience of that idea had him groaning.

O'Grady's eyes flashed and he growled like a dog. "I got my ticket-o-leave. Only got a year to go! I's as good as a free man. I ain't done nothing wrong! You're not taking me in!"

Sebastian rubbed his side and raised his brow. Even if the man was eligible for a conditional pardon, if he had not left the property to attend his ticket-of-leave musters, they would return him to service for that reason alone. "Since they issue a ticket after six years and you've been here for seven... that means you were sent out for fourteen years. So, your conviction was more serious than petty crime.

Technically, you are in possession of a fire-arm which is in direct breach of any ticket. Seems you may have missed a muster or two as well. These are not points in your favour. Although it matters to me not one iota whether you stay out of the work-gangs or not, it is entirely up to you. As of now: we are here to take legal occupation and that means you are trespassing. Please leave, so we can put this behind us."

Baker led out a bony sort of nag, saddled with an old frame of crusty leather that was cracking and fraying around the stitching. Sebastian presented it to him. "Consider this a farewell gift. No accusations of theft will be made. On your horse." He handed him the canvas bag from the buggy with some rations from their trip. "Don't camp within this boundary, or I *will* take you in for trespassing... squatting...loitering... holding a fire-arm... being a public nuisance... looking at me with a surly attitude. I don't care which."

He watched him ride off down the track. "Toms, I don't trust him as far as I can spit. Follow him... out past the boundary. Make sure he doesn't get distracted and decide to poison our water holes or something equally unhelpful."

Toms nodded. "Yes Boss."

Sebastian nodded and turned to Hannah. "Miss Hannah? I believe we were having an introductory tour before we were interrupted?" He held out his arm, but Hannah didn't move.

She blinked and took in a shaky breath. She wiped her sweaty hands down her sides and took another breath. "Oh. Yes," she said, as she bypassed taking his arm and walked up the stairs skirting very carefully the tobacco spit that dribbled down the verandah post.

He swallowed and said nothing but tucked in his elbow and followed her. He paused at the threshold with his hand on the knob ready to open the door. "Who knows what this is going to be like? I fear we need to prepare ourselves for something quite shocking."

Hannah nodded grimly. Sebastian opened the door and looked around. There was filth pervading every nook. Hannah gagged at buzzing flies crawling over a skinned possum frame hanging from a rafter over the table. She rushed down the stairs and was sick. Sebastian placed his kerchief over his nose and grimly surveyed the other rooms. There was some furniture that had obviously been left from a fairer time, but it was so basic or damaged that it evidently had not been worth selling off. Hannah stood by the gate, and waited for him there, muffling her gagging, by holding her sleeve over her mouth. He handed her his kerchief.

"You did well, Mr Digby, not to bring Lady Whitmore here. I'm sure I cannot sleep in there tonight."

"In there? Not a chance! The unpleasantness of an overnight hotel is one thing… bedding down under rotting game is another." He closed the gate firmly and it fell off in his hand. He propped it against the post. "We will make camp by the wagon for as long as we need to sort this out. We start tomorrow."

She raised her brow; surprised he had decided to stay the night. She fully expected him to immediately jump on the wagon and turn back. Back to… where though? They were marooned on a desert island called Australia.

"See if you can rally up some dinner while I do a walk around with Baker. Not sure if Toms will be back before sundown. We will keep him supper."

"Mr Digby?"

"Hmm?"

"I wanted to say that I think you handled that... ah... situation... with the squatter... I think you handled that well."

He grinned. "Well, you know me. Can talk-to-befuddle. Aunt Biddy always says that is my talent. Still, I'm glad we were able to avoid blood and blows. Mostly anyway," he said holding his side gingerly. He summoned Baker and they went off to inspect the sheds and stables. The outbuildings were, by all appearances, equally run-down and neglected, sections charred by the attempt to torch them.

They made camp on the dusty ground between the flat-bed dray and buggy. Penny and George had taught them to set up a camp kitchen on those long days when no settlement was in sight. Hannah – even if her name suggested it, was not a cook. She set the kindling and lit the fire. Dinner consisted of pan cooked fried potatoes and salted meat over an open fire. She boiled water for some tea... peat-bog variety. Life had been reduced to basic. Hannah knew Sebastian's inclination for pampering would be his undoing. This wouldn't last. And she was grateful she wouldn't have to wait very long before he pulled up stakes to go back to civilisation.

The sun was setting in a fiery blaze of red and gold that covered the massive sky around them. Sebastian swept his arm across the impressive canvas of stunning colour. "Never saw a sunset like this in England. This has the feel of a true adventure. How does it compare to the safari grounds of Whytehaven, Hannah?"

She paused and allowed herself to take it in. For a moment they had stepped inside a glorious theatre; the cathedral ceiling alight with the filtered hues of stained glass; the stage draped in swags of brilliantly dyed silk, the colours shimmering and changing and dancing. She felt the drama of the performance pulling her in. Some kookaburras burst out laughing, and dingos howled in the distance. "This is certainly colourful. A true safari."

He smiled into the depths of the fire. "Well, I am glad you are part of it. Aunt Biddy is grateful." He took a mouthful of the peat-bog tea, and swallowed deliberately as he looked at the fading colours on the horizon, quickly replaced by millions of sparkling star-lights. For a long time, he was unwilling to break the silence, as another sort of music lingered, and dallied, and tarried exquisitely. Eventually he sighed and quietly spoke. "Tomorrow the exploration of our new world continues. I naively thought it would be a simple matter of sweeping a few dusty boards and arranging our furniture tidily before we went to get Biddy. But it seems there will be more to it."

Hannah raised her brow. She was still convinced they would leave tomorrow, perhaps the next day. It would not be longer than that. She reminded herself again: housemaid-and-cook. "Yes, Mr Digby."

"Hannah, there is no one here to impress with your good manners. You can call me Sebastian."

"I would prefer to keep those lines clear, Mr Digby, now that…" She couldn't finish and she looked away.

"Now that... what?"

She really didn't want to get into it just now. Any appreciation of their glorious safari was squashed by the distasteful project before them. She felt tired and stressed and displaced. The reality of this country was every bit as harsh and unfriendly as all those accounts had purported it to be. "Now that I will never wear your ring."

"Never? What are you talking about?"

"I cannot. That is all."

"No, that is not all. What happened?"

"You seriously cannot be in earnest?"

The pained look in her eye sent him back to the inn... fogged by wine, loneliness, and rejection. A spark of clarity hit his chest. "Oh."

"Oh? That is all you have to say?"

"Hannah. Nothing happened."

"Oh, it happened. It happened entirely too much." She stood up and walked into the shadows. He followed her there.

"Okay. Okay. That happened. But nothing else. When I saw you deliberately flaunting your intention to keep company with your farmer, I was determined you would know what it felt like."

"He is not *my farmer*! We are not keeping company. I told you that!"

"Well, it didn't seem like it. I was going to... But when I got there, I couldn't do it. I just couldn't. I paid the fee and gave her the night off. I slept on the wagon. Ask your farmer."

"Not my farmer! Why would you tell me this? So, I know you intended to wound me? I saw that look. You knew it was like knives in my belly… and you pushed them in harder. You cannot deny it."

"Hannah, I don't remember too much, so I won't deny anything. But please know I am sorry for it. I am. But I cannot deny what happened later. I woke up lying on the canvas of the wagon, where your swag is… looking up at all these strange configurations of stars and constellations and I saw what this could be. I saw what *we* could be. This is exactly as you said all along. This is my adventure. Our adventure. This is it. I saw it all. It was incredible. Now that I know *that*, I'm not giving up on it. I cannot. And I will do what I need to do to have you join me in it."

"Well, that seems a little late and a little convenient, since I am here to do your bidding. But not as your wife. I will not be one who stands in public to watch such humiliation and shame flaunted so unapologetically."

"Hannah! We are not married. We are not even engaged. It seems entirely unfair that you can keep company with whomever you please, and yet you hold me to a standard that does not apply to yourself. I am free to talk to whomever I please, until you eliminate that forever."

"I was eating dinner with people I know. And you were not just talking. Don't make out you were."

"Hannah, tell me you will be mine… and all other doors are closed. Forever."

"Really? This is how you justify your shameless and wanton behaviour? None of that sounds like a potential suitor. Grief, you are unbelievable!" She turned away and climbed up over the wagon, to where the canvas covered load had become her bed. She squeezed her eyes closed and willed herself to sleep; the very place Sebastian confessed a revelation of destiny.

24.

A rooster crowed somewhere in the distance and the dawn light faded the shadows of the surrounding hills. Hannah stirred and rolled over trying to make sense of where she was. Her mind was fogged. She looked at the homestead as yesterday replayed in her mind. In that uncertain and dangerous moment as the musket exploded, Sebastian had not lost his composure. He had held his position. He had ingeniously talked him down, taking command of the situation. She looked at the campfire from on top of the wagon and watched him stirring the coals, fighting with the cooking pot that they used to boil water. But the smoothness of yesterday seemed to have melted in the morning heat. He swore as he burnt his forearm. Every task was clumsy and awkward. Where was the smooth rider; the skilled dancer; the jovial manipulator of cards? Another person from a lifetime ago. Toms appeared with an armful of cut wood and an axe over his shoulder. He banked the fired deftly and positioned the pot with ease. He spoke to Mr Digby in low tones, pointing around the layout of the farm.

Hannah climbed down and straightened her skirts and brown hair. She came around from the side of the wagon and nodded to the men. "Morning Ma'am," said Toms. Sebastian eyed him quickly, but he had already turned away and resumed tending the fire. They ate, balancing plates on their knees, and for a moment Hannah wished that Sebastian would make a quirky, droll joke and lighten the mood. But not to be. They knew what awaited them today, and nothing about that was remotely humorous.

Sebastian nominated that they start by dumping everything outside, and after that – scalding and scrubbing away the years of neglect and squalor. Once it was clean, they would proceed with unloading the wagon and moving in. They cautiously opened the door of the detached kitchen and looked around. Rats crawled over the rafters; junk jammed every available space. Some pans and utensils hung from hooks around the wall, and the hipbath jammed in there gathered tossed rubbish. They backed out in disgust and focused on the main house.

They started. The possum carcass came down and a scrawny dog, that they supposed had left with the Irishman, reappeared, and helped himself eagerly to the plunder. The table would go into stable tack room. Room by room the homestead was emptied to a shell. There were some surprises: books on a shelf that had evidently been an office; a drawer full of documents that seemed to have missed being tossed into the sea-trunk along with the other records; a bed frame or two, even though the mattresses were well and truly past usable. Stacks emerged of things they salvaged for the house. There were also stacks allocated for the shed; stacks of things to be repurposed; stacks of unusable junk to be dumped or burnt. Sebastian's eyes creased around the edges. "More piles to sort in my cabin, Miss Hannah? It is becoming a pattern."

His humour was like cool water in the warm weather. She responded eagerly with a smile. "This cabin has a little more space... but still your cabin, Mr Digby. I have experience with stacks." He nodded with a grin, and Hannah turned away, hiding her blush as she bundled more things into a pile. Why couldn't she stay mad at him? It would make it so much easier.

It took all day and still it was not finished. More experienced hands would have hardly called it an adequate day's work, but to this little crew it was an exhausting accomplishment. The next day… they did the same.

After dinner, they sat around their campfire fuelled with some of the broken junk that could not be fixed. Hannah looked into the flames, drinking her tea, and wondered about the practical dilemma of accessing hot water for tomorrow's clean-up. Sebastian raised his brow; the workings that provided hot water for his bath was a menial matter he had never had to bother with. He looked around at their faces and shrugged with a grin. "I confess I need your expertise to help solve this. We have a fire, but only small pots."

"There's the hipbath we found," Baker offered. "Still water-tight. I tested it because I thought I could use it to water the horses."

"Explain how this ingenious observation might actually be a workable solution?" Sebastian was not sure a tub that was to be put into service for something other than bathing was reasonable at all.

"We fill it from the well; put a fire under it. Like a copper."

"Copper what?"

"It's a laundry tub."

"Oh. That sounds completely unfathomable."

With that solution in place, Hannah retired to her swag. She was grateful she had priority place on the top of the wagon, and the protection it offered. They had heard the stories of snakes and spiders and giant lizards that were thicker than a man's thigh. She was reassured that this land did not have prowling lions, rampaging elephants, or the crazed hippopotamus of an African safari. And although she allowed for the exaggeration of an exciting tale, Australia's reputation demanded a healthy amount of respect.

Sebastian climbed up and sat at the end of her swag. "I like the view here. It is closer to heaven," he said looking at the stars.

"Would you like to swap places, Mr Digby?"

"No. I didn't come here to assert my right to be King of the Mountain. I wanted to ask your opinion on something."

"Oh. Okay..." She sat up. So, this would be the moment of confession: they were going to leave. Finally. He had stayed much longer than she thought his endurance could bear, but she was relieved it was over. It was impossible to imagine Lady Whitmore in such a place.

"What do you think of '*Whytefallow Downs*'?" She looked confused and said nothing. He stumbled a little, unsure of her silence. "Well... as a name for the farm."

"Hasn't it got a name?"

"Don't know. There was nothing on the deed or in the papers we went through. It feels like an abandoned child without an identity. But even if it had a name, anything my brother called it I would want to change."

Oh. Perhaps he held to the ethic of the Captain-in-charge who would stay with the condemned vessel until it sank. That was a surprise. She focused back on his question. "Why would you want to call it Whytefallow Downs?" she asked with a curious twist on her lips.

"As a tribute to Whytehaven... and all that means to me. This is too harsh to be a 'haven' and it seems kind of unfair to expect so much of it right from the start. But I am working on the idea of potential. Fields have the capacity to yield better after a season of fallow. I've been reading about the principle in Eddie's books. This place has had its fallow time... and now it's time to yield."

She started laughing.

"What?"

"I see what you are trying to do. It is even noble in its intent. But you can't call it that."

"Why not? Are you opposing me because of our personal differences? Is there a vindictive streak in your compliant exterior Hannah?"

"It is just... well... the name could be considered insulting. Not intentionally of course, but it has that tone."

"Biddy would not be insulted. Whytehaven was her home."

"True." She swallowed embarrassed. "But... Whytefallow sounds a lot like '*White-fellow*'. That is how the native aborigines talk about the colonisers. It is too close. The way people speak here... all slow and drawl, it could sound like White-fella..." She finished and turned her face away.

"Huh!" He turned it over in his mind: Whytefallow, White-fella, White-fellow. Yep, she was right. How did she even know that? "Okay. Well, I guess we are white fellows... and you probably have a point. Any other ideas?"

"I like the tribute to Whytehaven Hall. And I like the idea of fallow-ground. I'm not sure how to put it together."

"Fallowhaven Downs?"

"You said it wasn't a haven."

"Fallow-heights? What if we spelt it like Whytehaven with a Y: h-y-t-e-s. Fallowhytes."

"Hmm. Well, this place does have both hills and dales... like the fells and dells of Whytehaven."

"Hmm. The fallowed fields and the mountain heights. When it's run together it has Whyte in it too. Yes, I like that, pending Biddy's approval. No further ambiguity that is concerning the lady?"

She laughed. "I am suspecting this will be a place loaded with *ambiguity*, as you so aptly put it. It is one of the contradictory aspects of this strange new world."

He squeezed her ankle gently through her swag as he climbed down, rolling the name Fallowhytes over on his tongue. Hannah shook her head bewildered. He had named this? It was a sign of ownership that lot and portion numbers did not convey. It truly sent the signal that he was in; embracing the pain and uncertainty, challenge, and victory that this venture would bring. Something like anticipation rolled over in her belly. For the first time, she allowed the possibility that he had determined he would own this. Not just on paper. If he was in... how could she stand on the side-lines? She looked up at the night sky alight with a trillion, million stars and galaxies and tried to see the revelation Sebastian had been given.

Hannah woke with a start as a gunshot rang through the camp. She sat bolt upright in the dawn light, looking at

Sebastian standing there shirtless, pistol in hand, a large snake, dead, writhing at his feet. He picked it up by the tail triumphantly and looked up at her startled pale face. "Good morning, Miss Hannah!" he said cheerily as he displayed his trophy. George took it from him and chopped the head with an axe and flicked it onto the fire. They had heard that the bite of an Australian snake could drop a camel.

Sebastian reached over and gave his shirt a solid flick and pulled it on. She noticed the large bruise over his ribs where O'Grady had kicked him. By the time she climbed down, he was banking the wood on the fire. There was a little more confidence in the way he did that this morning.

Baker had found some eggs in the out shed, and as they cooked breakfast Sebastian turned to Hannah. "There is something I need you to do."

"Yes, Mr Digby?"

He frowned at her use of formal address, but let it go. "I want you to take shooting lessons."

"With a gun?"

"Yes. Both rifle and handgun. And before you assert you don't shoot and fetch: I need you to learn."

"Do you even know how to shoot? You said you never went hunting."

"I can shoot. Obviously," he said looking over at his morning trophy that was being dragged away by the dog, its mangy coat rough along its back. "I just do not shoot for entertainment that involves senseless torturing of the innocent. I have no such loyalty for matters of necessity. This is not entertainment. This may actually involve sustenance and survival here."

"I didn't even know you could shoot."

"We will have our first lesson while Toms and Baker set up the water for our clean-out today.   Right after breakfast."

"Now?"

"Yes.   It took more than one lesson to become a proficient dancer… so this will be our daily routine."

As she cleared up the breakfast things, she glanced over at him drinking his mug of tea. His face was rough with a morning shadow; his body animated as he was talking with Toms; his eyes bright with amusement from the discomfort of this bizarre inheritance.   How could this not dampen his humour? She almost believed that Sebastian had found his place.

When she finished washing the plates, he sat down beside her and handed her a pistol. He showed her how to feel the weight and balance in her hand. He described the various parts, and the mechanism. He showed how to load and unload. He stilled her trembling hands and guided them through the process. She could feel his closeness and she hoped he didn't realise it was not just the gun that was disturbing her. Kookaburras burst out laughing, mocking her lack of resolve and she put it down quickly. "I need a break," she said standing up and walking away.

"But we have only just started." He stood and paced around the fire. "Hannah, I know this is uncomfortable. But I need you to be safe. You got me here; now I need to be confident you are able to protect Aunt Biddy if we are away working in the paddocks. You may be here by yourselves at times."

"Oh. Okay." At least he thought her discomfort was just about the gun.

He looked at her. "For Aunt Biddy," he repeated reassuringly. And he went over to her and went through the loading procedure again. They walked away from the house, and he set a wooden block on a log. He paced back and stood behind her as he showed her how to sight it and aim… squeeze the trigger. He told her to anticipate the kick and held her arms firm against him as she squeezed her eyes shut and pulled. The report rang out, and she jolted. She stayed standing, hardly able to breathe, feeling his hands still supporting hers. Sebastian hadn't moved and was looking down at her. "You can open your eyes now," he said softly as he stepped away. "See? Just like dancing. And just like dancing you need to be able to do it with your eyes wide-open. You have to see what you are shooting at, particularly snakes. They move quick. But for a first lesson you have done well."

She seemed subdued as they walked back towards the homestead. Focus. "For Aunt Biddy…" she said quietly to the atmosphere. And Sebastian raised his brow with a grin. It was the first time he had heard her refer to Lady Whitmore without the use of her title. He took it as a sign: she was starting to see herself as family. That was progress.

⁂

They pulled out of the wagon stack all the buckets and things that could be used for scrubbing this hovel clean. There had been curtains on the windows in the back office – a room that was barely used by its recent occupant, and

Hannah had ripped them up into cleaning size rags and washed the dust and webs from them. She collected them from the verandah rail. Baker had found a few brooms with sparse bristles in the shed, along with a shovel or two. It was not a very convincing pile of weaponry, but Hannah had read in her Bible where Samson had waged war with the jawbone of a donkey. She decided that anything could be used effectively, given the right sort of energy.

So, they started the process of scraping out the rotting muck in the house. They scrubbed and scoured and washed the walls and the floors and the windows. George mended a fair share of floorboards, window sashes, railings, and the front step. Baker kept the supply of well-water up to the hipbath and the fire burning hot. Paint was a luxury they did not have access to yet, so they settled for clean. Very clean.

25.

The next morning as they sat around their campfire for breakfast, Sebastian made an announcement. "Shooting practice first thing, and then we finish cleaning and unloading the wagon. After that, I thought we would go visiting… to the neighbours."

"Visiting?"

"An entirely neighbourly thing to do. You and me."

"But Se… Mr Digby. You cannot take me visiting. I am in your employ."

"This is not my father's house. It will be fine if I say it is fine. We won't tell them that you are of the order of maids-and-cooks."

"But it is wrong to pretend it is what it is not."

"Just don't mention it then. You've done that before," he said with a grin. "I expect you to come… so you can feel the appropriate levels of obligation if that helps you to allow it. Besides, I'm thinking that here we can make it whatever we want."

She shook her head. "It will not do. I will only accompany you, if you disclose the nature of my position… and if we finish early enough so I have time to have a bath and change my dress."

He shrugged unperturbed. "I hardly see why we need to bother on both accounts, but whatever soothes your nettled conscience." And then with the driving energy of a squirrel preparing for winter Sebastian set everyone to work. What he anticipated would be an afternoon's sprint, turned into a marathon in league with the exertions of the Greek gods and ancient Olympic warriors.

Hannah was distressed that Lady Whitmore would be in a fever of anxiety since the timeframe to collect her would extend well past the week they had nominated for their return. So, Sebastian sent George into town to check on the couple and to reassure them of their progress. While he was away, together they scrubbed and cleaned, debating the best way to repurpose the things they had salvaged.

When they eventually started unloading, Sebastian dictated a system where Hannah directed the placement of pieces, so nothing needed to be handled twice. He put her trunk in the room next to the main bedroom allocated to Aunt Biddy. "Oh no," she objected, "that trunk is mine – it will need to go to the back room."

"This is your room. You need to be here next to Aunt Biddy. She has been unwell."

She looked around the large, airy space. "Mr Digby, it is more appropriate that you have this room."

"Why? I want the one next to the office."

"But Sir! That is not seemly. This is the better room."

"I am decided. I am not going to be tied to Aunt Biddy's side just because my brother demands she lives with me. That is your job and you won't be shirking on me."

"Sebastian! Don't you dare accuse me of shirking my responsibilities! You know I take my work seriously."

He considered her with a raised tilt of his brow, victorious that she had dropped her guard, and used his name. "Of course, you do: a serious room for serious house-staff. It has to be. That is all."

The overseer's hut was given the same intensive treatment. There was a squatting family of possums that had taken up residence. They were emphatically evicted as George was certain that Peggy would not cohabitate with them. But the family of possums returned and needed to be extracted again the next morning. Eventually the problem was solved by Baker experimenting with possum stew. It took a few days to sort his quarters as well, but finally, they had achieved a sense of order, at least with the accommodation arrangements for the new residents of Fallowhytes.

That next afternoon, Sebastian rigged up the buggy and took Hannah over to the neighbours. At Whytehaven Hall visiting neighbours was a twenty-minute jaunt. Here… they followed their directions on and on, and just as they were debating turning around, the gateway of Yellow Creek Station came into sight. The track up to the homestead also went on and on. When they pulled in, they were greeted with a level of reserved caution by the lady of the house. "Sebastian Digby," he offered, adding a happy explanation of their unannounced visit.

"I'm Winifred Elliot. Blake is expected back any moment." Visitors were unusual, but it seemed Winifred was soon reassured that this served to be a diverting afternoon. "Mr and Mrs Digby please join us for afternoon tea," she said extending the invitation to come inside.

Hannah tilted her head and turned to Sebastian. He simply replied in an offhand manner, "Oh no, Hannah is not my wife. My aunt requires some support, so Hannah has offered to combine managing the household with the needs of my Aunt. She is a family friend and indispensable in transitioning to our new life here."

Hannah waited for the gasps of shock, but Winifred simply smiled, obviously charmed by Sebastian. She nodded and opened the door with another very warm smile. Winifred offered them seats, set out the cups and poured the tea. "We all learn to diversify out here. Not much else we can do. I trust it will not take you long to settle in Hannah. How are you finding things so far?"

And so, the small talk began. Hannah glanced over the rim of her teacup to see if there was a sarcastic or scandalous edge to her seemingly embracing conversation. Admittedly Sebastian had managed to comply with her wishes still making her presence sound suitably respectable. Even so, she was surprised that Winifred Elliot looked comforted in having visitors regardless of the social strata they came from. Winifred apologised several times that Mr Elliot had not kept to his arranged timetable. They left with promises to come back Sunday-next for lunch, to meet Mr Elliot at a time when he was not out in the paddocks. They apologised again that they couldn't stay longer as tomorrow they were bringing Aunt Biddy home.

* * *

Aunt Biddy had lost weight, which gave her a gaunt, aged air. Sebastian assisted her up into the seat and Hannah climbed in beside her. Peggy sat at the back of the buggy, in amongst the packages of supplies they had bought while in town. Sebastian looked up at Aunt Biddy and wondered out-loud how she was going to manage the trip. "Don't fuss Sebastian. If I can get to some place that will afford a level of consistency – even if I can't hope for comfort, then I think that will be the best I can aim for. Just drive on and get me home."

Sebastian jumped up, clicked the reigns and moved out. "You call it home? Aunt Biddy you make some grand assumptions. It is a very basic set up. It is nothing like *home*."

"You know as well as I do Sebastian I am not going back. Whatever it is… that will be exactly what home looks like from now on. So, stop your apologising and keep those horses moving so I can see what fleapit shack is now to be my residing place until I take that final journey to my eternal resting place."

Hannah interrupted. "Oh, Aunt Biddy it is disturbing to hear to talk so! You know I will do all I can to attend to your needs and comfort. But Mr Digby is not exaggerating: it is basic and our best efforts may be in vain."

Aunt Biddy shifted her weight and smiled. "Oh, Hannah you are good for the soul. That day I interviewed you at Whytehaven, you were like a fresh breath of air. That inn! What a place." She lowered her voice and lent in towards Hannah. "I thought I would positively waste away from boredom once I started to feel better. I've decided there is such a thing as being too agreeable."

"I don't want to be *dis*agreeable Aunt Biddy," said Hannah with a frown.

"Pish-posh and twaddle my dear. Disagreeable just means you trust me enough to be honest. Now tell me, why do you now call me Aunt Biddy… which I have never heard you do before… and you have reverted to calling Sebastian

'Mr Digby'… which I find ridiculously formal given your status in the family."

"Oh Lady Whitmore! I am so sorry. I have been presumptuous."

"Rubbish. I do not object. In fact, you started it, so from here on in I will not answer to any 'Lady Whitmore' nonsense. It is decidedly un-colonial. Aunt Biddy it is."

"But Lady Whitmore, I do not think that is at all appropriate."

Aunt Biddy turned deliberately to Sebastian who had the most curious smile around his eyes, and they collaborated to intentionally ignore Hannah's use of title. "So, Sebastian, do you think that you can make this little bird you call a farm, take wing and fly? What does the place need to get some life and lift out of it?"

"Huh! If only I knew. I am going over the farm with Toms, but there is barely anything left. A caretaker was never appointed. We had to evict a squatter, who looks like he only ever lifted a finger to shoot enough game to survive. The more Toms shows me, it is evident the whole place was stripped bare when Roderick left. We know they used to run sheep, although there were no records relating to that side of the farm. We found some other records in a drawer in the office, and there may be more information to be discovered there. We have a shearing shed and yards of sorts… but the equipment is gone. Not that it makes much difference, because there is no livestock; and I don't know the slightest thing about a woolly wether anyway."

"So, you are researching? That is good."

"My research is hardly helpful... except perhaps I can acknowledge the potential still stands. If they did it once, surely, we can do it again. In fact... you are right... I'm counting on it."

"There! Mr Digby is not going to be just an ordinary farmer. He is going to be a sheep farmer," said Aunt Biddy half to herself and half to Hannah with a hint of mischief.

"Don't do that. It will drive me insane if I have to listen to two women call me Mister."

"Hush Sebastian. I am only teasing. It has been entirely too long where I couldn't tease anyone without causing either the greatest offense, or overwhelming confusion. It is good to be back where the world is as it should be. Family being family." She turned to Hannah. "And yes, that includes you."

"Yes, Aunt Biddy..."

"Good girl. Now don't forget," she said has she patted Hannah's knee contentedly and slipped into a dozing sort of silence hanging on as they rocked and rolled over ruts in the track, headed towards home.

* * *

26.

"Now Aunt Biddy, don't panic. It is clean, even if it is rather drab. We have scrubbed this place top to bottom. We will get to the painting in time."

She raised her brow. "Really? Scrubbing? I can't imagine Sebastian scrubbing anything, except his manicured fingernails."

Sebastian frowned; Hannah saw a shadow cross his eyes and she instinctively went to his defence. "Ma'am, I feel I need to exonerate Mr Digby and explain he did his fair share in preparation for your homecoming. He is learning to adapt. He has even gone hunting with more than a notebook and a spy-glass."

"Oh, I am not surprised. Sebastian is the original little chameleon… those amazing exotic little creatures that turn to whatever their environment demands of them. He will make the most capable sheep baron, producing the finest wool in Australia. The anticipation just now, is how he will accomplish this plan."

Sebastian just chuckled. "You are still delirious from your sickness, Aunt Biddy. I have no plan."

She smiled unperturbed. "Not yet… but your mind is grinding overtime to find one that will work. It will come."

"Well, if you have any divine insights on how that might be accomplished, please don't hold back. I have no notion what I am doing, or where to start. It is ridiculous that we have a farm, and no plan."

"Well, perhaps *you* are the plan. Perhaps you just need to start…"

Even to Sebastian's rather adaptable mind this venture seemed beyond ludicrous.

"Just do whatever is next. Start doing that."

Hannah cleared her throat and stepped down from the cart. "Well, we can start with having some dinner and settling you in. You have the best room in the house, Aunt Biddy. The doors open onto the verandah and there is a lovely view across the paddocks to the hills."

"Ahh. The Fallowed Heights. Well, I think that dinner is a perfect place to resume life together… without something moving under my feet… be it ship-decking, or horse-carriages, or the floorboards of rickety old inns. I am looking forward to acquiring the stability of my land-legs."

With that, she leant heavily on Hannah's arm as she was led up the front stairs to the verandah. She stood at the front door and looked slowly around the main living room.

"Did you want the tour now or in the morning, Aunt Biddy?" asked Hannah softly.

"Later will be fine, Dear. I am not going anywhere." Hannah guided her to her room. Aunt Biddy paused momentarily at the door of her bedroom, took a deep breath and pursed her lips. "Hmm. I am going to lie down. Hannah, call me when dinner is served."

Hannah glanced at her concerned. She closed the door behind her, and tears stung the back of her eyes. For someone Sebastian's age, she expected, even demanded, that this would be an adventure… a challenge of adaptability. But for someone of Lady Whitmore's age and station, she was suddenly aware how cruel and humiliating this ruling was. Sebastian put her portmanteau near her door quietly and raised his brow in query. Hannah shook her head and swallowed hard. She excused herself quickly went out the back and checked that Peggy was starting dinner and then bustled to the dining room to set the table. Sebastian followed her there.

"Is she not well yet?" he asked quietly.

"She is well enough… but this place…" She shrugged, despairing. "This is not adequate for her station and what she is used to. It is an awful thing to expect. I've tried to make it comfortable with the few things that we have. But her heart is breaking for home. I had forgotten how strong the pull of home must be."

"What can we do?"

"I don't know. I really don't know."

He looked at her. "She will want us to get along. Family is home for her too."

"Sebastian. This is not about us. My mind is not changed."

"I know it is not changed. Not yet."

"Not ever!" she said fiercely under her breath, her eyes flashing.

"We can and will get along. I expect it." She turned away but he went around and stood in front of her. "Hannah, I demand it. Do not underestimate how serious I am about this. Aunt Biddy will see us – if not as admirers… at least as friends. Good friends. More than employer and servant. You have to understand my expectation here."

"You cannot force me to be your friend!"

"I can."

"How? That is ridiculous."

"The tenet is on respect, open exchange, kind conversation and regard. You do that… or you can leave."

"You cannot dismiss me! I am in Lady Whitmore's employ."

"Unfortunately, you are now in my service. Your Lady Whitmore does not have the financial resources to employ." He shrugged. "Neither do I – the truth be known. And you can leave if you wish. I am not going to chain you as if you are in a prison. But I propose you stay. Respectfully. As a friend, and we find a way to give you what is owed. Perhaps shares in the property. Have you ever been a landowner, Miss Hannah?"

"Are you offering a partnership… without marriage?"

"I am."

"How long have you known that you don't have the income to support staff? I thought you were still provided your allowance."

"Well… I'm increasingly doubtful that money will ever come through, regardless of what was pledged. Particularly if they believe the content of that letter, be it true or not."

"What about George and Peggy?"

"They are here on a board-and-lodging arrangement. Wc have started with a slx-month term. If they want to leave after that for a more comfortable position, they will go with a solid referral. It was a way to guarantee their passage. To avoid questions. Although, I do admit, the expectation of any interrogation was a little overstated. The same applies to Baker."

"When did you know?" she repeated.

"On the ship. Not before, I swear. As I was going through the ledgers."

"Why did you not say anything then, or since?"

"And say what? *Oh, by the way… you are unemployed and destitute… like my good self. Sorry about that: you left everything you have ever known, to come to nothing.* I thought marriage would justify it somehow, but you are determined not to. And that is your choice. But, Hannah, we can do this! I know we can, but not as enemies. I need you on side. Aunt Biddy needs you on side."

She sat down and ran her hand up over her hair that was tied back in a bun. "So, what are you offering?"

"The same terms you had at Whytehaven. We will keep records and allocate a quarterly equivalent as shares in the property, up to a third allocation. You also get a voice on decisions that impact the property and what happens here. I will retain the right of veto."

"I really have no choice, do I?"

"You always have a choice. That is the point."

"But the choice you offer is like your father's: do this or become enamoured with the lifestyle of a market-square beggar."

He understood the accusation and shrugged. "I can't and won't force you to stay. But if you do, Hannah, it will not be as a maid and a cook. It will be as a friend and a partner. Unless of course you change your mind and marry me… which I am still open to considering."

"Sebastian Digby, in some way this feels devious and conniving. But I have nothing that would make such an accusation stick. So, I guess you are right: friends we are."

"Excellent! Friends." He looked so very pleased. "No more 'Mr Digby' nonsense. We will tell Aunt Biddy the good news at dinner."

"I will call you Mr Digby if I please. And since we are not getting engaged, it hardly deserves a formal announcement."

"Believe me – she will be encouraged by the arrangement."

27.

They sat around the table and bowed their heads while Sebastian said grace. He flicked the serviette onto his lap with practiced ease. Aunt Biddy paused and watched him before she took up her spoon. "It is something of a relief to be sitting together around our own table again."

Hannah nodded. "I'm glad you think so. You will be pleased that I did not have sole responsibility over the kitchen tonight. I'm grateful Peggy is back to look after dinner."

Aunt Biddy ate her soup in silence. Sebastian cleared his throat. "Aunt Biddy, I will apologise now. There will be some noise first thing in the morning: I am teaching Hannah how to shoot. Just before breakfast is the best time – it doesn't interfere with the rest of the day."

"Shooting? With a gun?"

"Yes, Ma'am. It is Mr Digby's opinion that I am in need of expanding my skill set. For protection. We are quite isolated here."

"I assumed isolation would be its own protection. Am I wrong?"

"Aunt Biddy, we had to evict a squatter when we arrived… an unsavoury sort. Apparently, the underbelly of society that is the reputation of the colony exists even out here and may find their way to our door. Then there is the wildlife factor. Not sure what poses the greatest danger, but better to be equipped just in case."

"So, Hannah what is your best score?"

"Score? What do you mean?" asked Hannah with a frown.

"Oh come. I am confident Sebastian hasn't altered his entire personality, just because he has changed his shirt and no longer lives in a dinner jacket. If he is teaching you to shoot, there will be score-keeping involved. Am I wrong? Has this been overlooked?"

Hannah laughed and put down her spoon. "You are so right, Aunt Biddy. Competitive to the core. I achieved three clean shots out of ten yesterday morning. I am only learning."

"And you, Sebastian? Are you still as adept as when you were shooting the Academy championships?"

"Championships?" said Hannah, swallowing her soup a little too quickly and she spluttered ungainly. "Have you been feigning your scores to allow me to feel better about learning?"

"I might be out of practice?" he suggested with smirk.

"Oh, that is too much! I do not need your sympathy to learn a new skill. I am quite capable of swallowing my pride to improve." She took a drink of water and coughed again.

"Very well then, Hannah. All charitable considerations are here by suspended. We will see how long it takes you to match me shot for shot. Aunt Biddy you may be called on to adjudicate once more."

She shrugged with a shake of her head. "As long as it is good natured practice and not unbridled warfare. I trust you know the difference."

"Aunt Biddy! That you would suggest such a thing! If Hannah can match me to eighty percent within four months… she will have her chance to demand of me anything she chooses. Same reward as Feather, Furred, and Flowered. Do you accept this challenge?" He stood up and wrote the details on a piece of paper and put it on the mantlepiece. The date stared at her, teasing.

"You've just disclosed being a shooting champion. You think I have no chance, and I will be in your debt again. But there is a competitive streak in my personality that may surprise you, Mr Digby."

"Really? You have insisted on no tallies in previous games. That sounds entirely indifferent to the idea of competition." He smirked and finished his soup. *'Oh, I am not surprised,'* he thought to himself. *'Not at all! Just take the bait Hannah… come on, just a nibble,'* he urged silently in his head.

Hannah tilted her head. "Consider yourself matched… to ninety percent," she declared as she stood up to clear the soup plates and went out to help Peggy serve the next course.

Aunt Biddy reached over and patted Sebastian's hand. "You do me good Son. We will make this work. It will be okay."

He nodded and stared after Hannah. "It will be more than okay. She has agreed to working for a partnership. Step one. Daily coaching in shoot outs… step two."

"Her agreeing to come was step one. You are determined. But so is she. It is what this place needs."

"Perhaps we came here to eliminate the social divide. No one honestly cares about that here. Our neighbours were quite unmoved by the declaration of our status or lack of it."

"Neighbours?"

"Yellow Creek Station. The Elliot woman talks like an antique, but she can't be that old. We go visiting again on Sunday to complete our neighbourly introductions, to her husband. And I have some things I'm inclined to discuss if he proves to be the discussing type. I have made a resolution to avoid business the traditional Digby way… in manner and associates. I want to avoid my father's sort altogether."

"And if it becomes unavoidable working with those of your father's temperament… be confident that you know what to expect and you will be alert to their devious agendas. If nothing else, Sebastian, your background has sharpened your wits and made you wise."

"Wise? No one has ever accused me of wisdom before. Shallow and irresponsible perhaps," he said with a chuckle.

"The lack of recognition doesn't mean it isn't there. Eddie said that about you – *'Sebastian has more smarts about him than most men I know; and wise enough to hide a few cards into the bargain'.*"

He laughed. "Aunt Biddy! You sound proud that Eddie accused me of being a conniving cheat! What about all those integrity speeches?"

"It is not cheating if you hold the cards in your hand and not up your sleeve. The metaphor is imperfect, but you know what I mean. Take it slowly until you know who your players are."

"Always, Aunt Biddy. Always."

Hannah and Peggy arrived with the main meals. It was sparse in variety, but still it had the feel of home as they sat and talked. The process of becoming familiar with the unfamiliar had begun.

28.

They pulled up outside Yellow Creek homestead; Sebastian jumped down and gallantly assisted the ladies to alight. Sunday lunch was substantial. Hogget was on the menu and a pleasant change from salted beef or the strong taste of Australian native game, which had been their staple since their arrival at Fallowhytes.

After lunch, the ladies brought out their sewing projects and sat around tea, chatting about family and solutions to frustrating situations they encountered. Hannah soaked up this local wisdom of remedies and recipes like a dry sponge. She was doing her own research.

Sebastian retired to the office with Blake Elliot. They sat over a glass of scotch. It was a relief to Sebastian to be in the company of someone, who even in the rough and tumble of this place, had time for quality comforts. As he swirled the amber liquid, he settled in to *get to know the player.* He started by asking if he thought the valley was a good place to raise a young family.

Blake paused and then raised his glass amiably. "Raise a family? I would not know. Winifred is my sister, so she is the only 'Elliot family' I have here, and it has been a comfort to have her join me. She has not long moved out here to manage the household."

"Well family does come in all forms," said Sebastian with a grimace. Speaking of siblings, he asked whether Elliot had dealings with his brother Roderick before he left. Apparently, he had already left by the time Elliot came to the valley.

181

Blake queried about the squatter O'Grady, and Sebastian, in his very unassuming way of making the understated an exciting story, told him how he was evicted on arrival. Elliot enjoyed the yarn and then shrugged. "He was a tough old bugger. Had quite the reputation of hermit. Couldn't run any of my sheep on those borderlands of yours even though it was begging to be pastured. He would just peg them off like flies. No doubt he'd eat some, but he'd just shoot at the rest. In the end I just told my guys to avoid your boundary."

"So, are you interested in grazing my land?" ask Sebastian as he swirled his drink. Ideas were swirling in his mind.

"I need the pasture."

"Well, you've probably guessed, I don't come from a sheep background. And even if I did, this is very different from English country. So, there's no pretending I know what I'm doing. There are things here that don't make sense." Sebastian shrugged frankly. He didn't want to let on that his research to date consisted of books from Eddie's out-dated library and a farmer named George. He had marked Blake Elliot as his next library-book project, full of information to be read. He needed to understand farming, and the way it was done here. "My brother treated that place like a brothel and had no qualms about stripping it naked; raping it; and then he up and left. But you've got a different style about you, Mr Elliot. My land's been fallow for seven years now and I've got pasture you could use. We can settle the agistment in payment of live-stock, and a percentage of the woolclip at the end of the shearing."

"Digby, you really must be the village idiot. No one does business that way."

Sebastian knew that if Elliot believed he was ignorant and gullible, or just plain stupid, he would not feel threatened by his intention to rebuild. People are not guarded if they think they are smarter. O'Grady was evidence of that. The high-society players he used to rub shoulders with were exactly the same. "Hmm… maybe. Or… maybe it isn't done that way, until someone does it that way. Cash payments are just going to flag Roderick's creditors that I'm here, and I need time. You don't think this is fair?"

Elliot looked at him while he drank. "Doesn't seem like there's enough in it for me," he said frankly. Sebastian saw Elliot consider his visiting clothes and the blisters on his soft hands as he looked over the rim of his drinking glass. And Sebastian suspected Elliot was calculating how to take this naïve clean-skin for more.

Sebastian happily allowed the misconception to play out, as he sat, and drank, and talked rubbish. He found an idea forming. Yes, he needed time. Time to learn sheep farming. Time to restock. Time to restructure confidence with creditors. Time to rebuild what had fallen over or had been demolished in Roderick's malicious exit. Time to prove himself to Hannah. He could learn from Elliot under the guise of a farmhand who had no energy to be a farmer in his own right. Sebastian coolly took another drink and made a joke. Yes, now he had the makings of a plan.

"I'll tell you what. I'll work for you: four days in the week. I don't want to work full time, but I reckon a cheap extra hand should add to the balance." Sebastian's assessment was that Elliot was reasonable, but even he probably wouldn't hesitate to step on another's back to progress. That was another thing just like home: the landed sector are an ambitious lot. In a frank moment of acknowledgement, Sebastian could even admit that observation applied to him now. They shook hands and signed the paper. Review it in a year.

Sebastian had no idea how long he would need to accomplish those things he had set himself. After all, without purpose, more 'time' just makes you older. He knew he had at least six months with George, Peggy, and Baker as a resource. Twelve months learning and working under Elliot. He wanted Fallowhytes to have full advantage of George's farming know-how, so together they started. They planted a vegetable garden, began repairing out-buildings, brought in cattle that had been running in the back hills for seven years, started breaking-in a house cow or two; clearing paddocks for cropping; and housing the poultry that had been roaming feral so that there was a regular supply of eggs for the household. The income Sebastian received from Elliot was nothing to speak of, so they had to be as self-supporting as possible.

At the beginning of the week, Sebastian rode off in the dark to work at the Yellow Creek spread. He stayed over there and allowed himself to be the butt of all sorts of useless, green, fancy-pants, silver-spoon jokes. The upside was that they could not beat him at cards, and in lieu of money, he would sometimes trade winnings for answers to practical questions. He didn't want to seem too nosey, so he played the dumb English aristocrat card just enough to mask his intentional up-skilling aspirations. The days were long, and hard, and exhausting. But the observing and the learning kept him going back. When he returned to Fallowhytes, he worked with George the same long hours. They would talk about the way things were done 'next-door' and how George had solved problems back in England, and how this could be adapted in working Fallowhytes' future.

29.

Hannah woke with anticipation. Today was a home-day. She lit the lamp, brewed a pot of tea, and set it on the table. When Sebastian emerged from his room crumpled and scruffy, she sat with him and noticed how comfortable it was to sit in the silence across from him. And she also noticed how uncomfortable it was at the same time. As the weeks merged into the next, the Sebastian who once was immaculate in his dress, and couldn't take anything seriously… was now careless about the creases on his pants and was gravely immersed in sensible work.

He watched her pour his cup of tea and wondered out loud what it would be like to grow and harvest tea-leaves, to compensate for their colonial deprivation. "It is a hardship that the English outposts in India or Ceylon have never had to endure. We may even earnestly satisfy the palates of discerning gentlemen and surpass the legend of the Malayan blends."

Hannah chuckled. These moments fanned her heart like live coals in a hearth that refused to go cold. She never anticipated that she'd miss his droll banter and his unsolicited attentions. But he didn't grin over his joke. "Oh. You are serious," she said in surprise.

"I think it is well established that tea is a very serious matter," he said with twist on his lips that complimented the slightest glint in his eye.

"I guess this means we may be exploring the idea of a cultivation paddock with a fair selection of tea bushes in the future."

"We may develop a reputation of raising the level of refinement in this uncivilised corner of the Empire." Then he did raise his brow and grinned openly.

Why was it that every little detail about him seemed to be magnified: his stance, his frown, the crinkling around the edges of his blue eyes when he smiled, the way he sat in a saddle, and the tired slump of his shoulders when he came in after dark. But she could not let him know how it was for her. He seemed to have settled into a state of comfortable acceptance that life here at Fallowhytes was his lot and destiny. But this acceptance was not resignation. She saw how hard he was working at this.

Sebastian picked up his cup and finished his tea and didn't say much until they walked out together for their shooting practice. They had established the spot as a rifle-range. What used to be an odd assortment of objects propped along a log, were now bracketed targets along the stand of trees at varying distances. Each board had graduated scoring sectors. "So, Hannah. How is your line of sight this morning?"

"Tolerable enough."

He watched her as she loaded and shot. "You hold your hand steady. You stare down your aim with focus. There is no hesitation with your trigger touch. Your shot it is firm and smooth."

"The scrutiny is unnecessary, Sebastian. The measure of my improvement was to match a percentage of your scores. I am getting closer."

"Indeed, you are. You are so improved; you must be practicing while I am away."

"I don't recall any prohibition on that. I also have a growing tally of snakes, chicken hawks, and possums to my belt. The timeframe you set for your challenge means I still have time before the final shoot-out. I am determined to match you."

"Well, you have declared the rules mean I cannot fudge my performance, so I think it has the makings of an exciting contest."

They sat at the table in the shed while they oiled the guns and put them away in the case. "You did not disappoint. You have been ruthless in your determination to best me," said Sebastian.

"So, you honestly declare that you did not accommodate me in this win?" she asked sceptically.

"I missed a couple of basic shots. I declared up front I was tired, yet you would not flex the date that was set."

"You determined the time of the contest, and that may have been my only advantage. Even though I feel the edge of your competitiveness seems a little blunt this morning, I have resolved to enjoy it anyway."

"Do you enjoy the win… or the proficiency obtained in the execution of your duties… or the knowledge of besting me?"

"Winning with a prize is the bonus. As I recall it was your expectation that I be competent in protecting Aunt Biddy while you are away. Of course, I want to do that well. You know me. Always sensible."

"You take sensible so seriously."

"If I didn't, it wouldn't be sensible."

"So, what will it be? What service will you demand as your prize? Will your reward be something as simple and menial as stowage? That seemed to be the pinnacle of your ambitions when we first played *Feathered or Furred*."

She laughed. "Oh Sir, you forget nothing! But I have no need to waste such a trump card on stowage now. Rather I have something much more sensible in mind. Come, it is breakfast time."

"Surely you don't mean that we eat breakfast together? Will you not choose something more noteworthy for your prize?"

"Of course, I will. This is just breakfast – the same as always. I will choose something less usual for my prize." She picked up the case with the handgun and started to walk towards the house.

"So, it is unusual? You torment me! You do know that there is a statute of limitations on when you can extract your prize."

"Of course. One week. I am very aware."

For two days Sebastian hounded Hannah for a description of his obligation. "Why not tell me? That would be sensible even. I go away tomorrow. I will not see you for four days. By then your week expires."

She laughed. "But if I tell you now, it spoils the fun. Hold on to your hat Sebastian. I promise I will let you know before the day is out."

He stared at her, mesmerised, as he sat at the breakfast table. "Is this Hannah... tormenting me with the excuse of fun? *That* hardly seems sensible."

"It was your assertion that we bring each other balance. You are working long, hard hours so perhaps this is my way of offering a counter-weight."

"Just tell me what my obligation is. I would prefer it."

She put down his bowl of porridge and sat down opposite to him. "I'm sure you would."

"You have no intention of telling me! How can I offer my service if I have no information?"

She sat down. "Well alright. I have decided on…" She shook her head and picked up her spoon. "No. I wish to eat my breakfast uninterrupted by your haggling over the appropriateness of my choice. You will have to wait."

Hannah went out to the shed where Sebastian and George were sorting through discarded implements to try and put together some sort of working version of a plough. They fixed up the old forge to work the metal into useable parts. She put down a basket of biscuits and bread, and the curious Australian billy-can that was the perfect invention for making tea outside of civilized parlours. She filled it with water and put it on the edge of the forge to boil.

"It appears we are banned from coming inside when we look like this?" said Sebastian as he wiped his hands of soot and grime on a rag.

"Of course. I would not be accused of interrupting your work for long."

"So, sensible Hannah, have you put 'disclosure' on the menu? Is that why you are here? Normally you would send

Peggy with the morning tea. Are you going to tell me what I am obligated to deliver as your prize?”

She was enjoying this diversion, and chuckled while she added tea leaves to the billy. She watched Sebastian wash his hands in a bucket and then munch on a biscuit. “Hmm? No. I don’t think I will tell. It would be too distracting. You have so much work to do before you leave in the morning.”

George rolled his eyes and gabbed a biscuit. “Gee! This is like the torture of watching a travelling village pantomime,” he said under his breath. “Kill me now!” he added, and he went out the back of the shed to rifle through some junk looking for a suitable piece of steel for his project.

“I need another tack,” Sebastian said under his breath, ignoring that jibe. His badgering hadn’t worked so far. But Hannah was gently flirting, and it had his attention. “If I do not know your request before I leave tomorrow morning I will be off the hook. One week – that is the rule. I will not put off going to Elliot’s. Even though he thinks I am just there because I have no motivation to farm my own place. It is my way to immerse myself in the learning of it.”

“The week is not yet expired. I am obligated to let you know what I have nominated as my prize. Your obligation is to find a way to start. You cannot delegate. I have won a service exclusively from you. That is the challenge. Once it is started, you can take as long as you need to complete it.”

“So, you are saying that if I just *start* before the week is out, that will be sufficient to meet the parameters of this obligation? Then I can finalise it at my leisure? I feel your previous inflexibility over the rules has suddenly become quite pliable... to your advantage." He turned away and pumped the bellows to fire up the forge. He didn't want her to see he was pleased she was haggling over the rules. He was grateful he missed those shots. This was reward enough.

All during dinner he looked expectantly as she ate her soup, and cut her meat, and drank her tea. Still, she carried on blithely in her conversation. After dinner Sebastian sat for a short while but was soon nodding off in his chair. "Ladies, I must abandon this attempt at social civility, because in reality I am being entirely anti-social. I'm off to bed. Good night."

"Good night, Mr Digby."

"If you are sure...?"

"I am sure it is a good night."

"But...?"

"Good night."

He sighed. More than just fatigue. All day he had been so hopeful that her playfulness was a sign that she was open to his attentions, and that the service she would choose would be something less mundane... something akin to a date. It was ironic and frustrating that this hope would come when he neither had the time nor the energy to do it well. That was surely not fair. As she sat sewing, as if in the drawing room of Whytehaven, chatting with Aunt Biddy on a choice of vegetables for their newly turned garden bed, he acknowledged he had been entirely too optimistic. Perhaps all it showed was the type of changes this new situation brought. After all, vegetables would never have been a topic of conversation in that other life.

He washed up in the bowl on his washstand and turned back the covers of his bed. As he did, a folded sheet of paper on his pillow fluttered to the floor. He picked it up and read it with a raised brow:

"No frivolous services I choose for my prize,
The petition I desire to try on for size:
Tutored lessons, saddled horse-back rides,
Coach my equestrian efforts; improve and advise.
H."

Hmm. What could he make of that? Unexpected. Sensible… Now that shooting practice was more or less obsolete, had she conjured up another excuse to be coached by him? More dancing in time? That made him smile.

He went into his office and wrote a note in reply. When he left in the morning dark, he folded it and placed it under her teacup on the table:

"The risk you take in writing your request nearly went unnoticed. Fortunately, your note was found. You require lessons in horse riding from me? So very sensible Hannah! I am at your service.
In a reduced situation, where stable hands are not common, a rider must become skilled in care of tack and animal husbandry. Your first lesson is to oil a saddle and bridle. The equipment is old, so it may need the treatment a number of times. Baker will help you if you have questions. No delegation implied; he is a resource for a recognised provision of service. S."

Hannah read it and took a deep breath. She had insisted on sensible, but now that Sebastian was consumed with driving sensible duties, she wondered if his ambition had overtaken him, and she was not important to him at all. Yet he had responded. He was not too busy. Not too tired. He had not considered this too trivial to participate.

She went over to the stable and Baker pointed to a saddle laid out with oil and rags. She stared at it in confusion. "Baker? This is not… well… it is not a ladies' saddle. Surely, he doesn't think that I am to ride that?"

Baker made no attempt to understand. "No idea, Ma'am. I only know that he wanted me to show you how to wash and oil it. Perhaps he is going to use it for himself?"

Well, that made no sense. He already had a preferred saddle. But she had appointed Sebastian as her tutor, so as the pupil she was obligated to follow the instructions he offered. After she had thoroughly washed down the saddle, Baker insisted it needed to dry for at least a couple of days.

Then during the day, in between her other routines, she went over to the stable and rubbed oil into the thirsty leather. As she sat, massaging the oil in, it became more than merely extracting a service as a prize. It was massaging her dry emotions supple again. When Sebastian rode up late that evening, she was still sitting in the stable, oilcloth in hand. He unsaddled and brushed his mare down, fed her; then he came over and sat down beside Hannah. "So, the victor wants riding lessons. That was unexpected. I thought you rode at Whytehaven often enough to claim adequate expertise."

"You know I cannot ride. That outing was probably the third time I had ever sat in a saddle. No wonder my very first *'Feathered or Furred'* tally looked so poorly. I had to focus intensely on riding the horse – even at an ambling stroll... Oh!”

“Oh?”

“You knew! That is why you insisted we went walking on our next excursion. You were saving me from the indignity of having to ride again.”

“You give me too much credit Miss Hannah,” he said with a smile.

“My point being, my short experience with horses does not qualify as competence. Not in any way that is useful at least.”

“Ahh. The sensible, practical, useful Hannah once more.”

“There is nothing wrong with sensible. I want to be able to help you around the farm. I can do that better if I can ride.”

“Then I was right. You will need to ride astride.”

“Astride? So, this saddle is for my use? I cannot ride something like *this*!”

“You have followed my instructions methodically so far. Just keep doing that and we will have you riding steeplechases in no time.” He chuckled as he inspected her work, running his finger over the surface. “It is possible this saddle has been oiled so thoroughly it will slide right off the horse’s back.”

“Are you saying I have failed this lesson?”

“I was applauding your enthusiasm. You’ve done a commendable job. The challenge of neglected equipment is that it needs more work to make it serviceable. I’ll take particular effort to strap the girth tightly to mitigate slippage.”

"Oh. Well..." She stood up, embarrassed for some unfathomable reason. "Welcome home, Mr Digby."

"Home. I like the sound of that. I'll wash up... and meet you over at the house... at home."

The next morning, Sebastian insisted that they continue their usual shooting practice so that her progress would not wane. Hannah looked at him with a narrowed gaze as they walked back to the stables. "You seemed to have regained your accuracy with the targets this morning."

Sebastian shrugged as they put away their rifles. "I slept well. We are only judged on crossing the line on race day. Are you ready for a morning ride?"

"Surely not yet! I have only just started rubbing down saddles. Are there not more technical aspects that I need to become familiar with first?"

"Just like dancing and shooting, doing is the best tutor."

"It was a silly idea. I shall withdraw my request."

"It was a completely sensible idea. It was agreed that should I start before the week's end it would be locked in. I met that challenge... even though you did all you could to sabotage my participation. So, you cannot renege. I am obligated to be your tutor until you are accomplished." He shrugged and didn't look at all perturbed that such a commitment was required of him.

She sighed. "But what if I cannot learn?" The horse standing in the stall seemed entirely too intimidating.

"Then you are doomed to be bound to me as a student for ever and ever." He grinned as her eyebrows shot up high. "We will ride until you master this. That should be motivation enough for you to quickly become proficient." He picked up his hat and walked with her to the house. "After breakfast, I have to catch up with Toms briefly, but then we will start. I want to begin riding the boundary today, so you can come with me for the first part."

"Out there? In the paddocks? Oh, that is not a good idea. Can't I ride in the closed holding-yard instead? These horses are not the placid geldings of Whytehaven."

"It is a perfectly suitable mission. Shepherds are obsolete out here. Fences are needed if we are going to run livestock. We have a couple of fences on bordering property lines, and I need to start mapping what needs fencing. Riding a boundary is entirely an appropriate learner activity."

"Aunt Biddy might need me."

"Peggy is available. I can pull rank. I could do that since this is my farm."

"I thought you said I would have a say."

"Very well. Your say today will be in finding some clothes that will allow you to ride across a saddle – like a man. Your previous riding habit probably won't work."

When she arrived at the stables, he looked her up and down. "As pretty as you look, I fear you did not do well on this assignment. You cannot possibly wear that."

"What do you mean? I know it is not new, but I was assured this riding habit was a very practical choice. It has leggings, and fullness in the skirt. I'm sure it will do."

"Hmm. Come here. Don't move."

"Why?"

Sebastian pulled out a knife and slit her skirt down the middle, from her thigh to the hem.

"What are you doing? Are you insane?"

"Turn around." He spun her about and did the same to the back in a single deft move. "There you are. That should solve the problem readily enough."

When she turned back her face was white with indignation.

"Don't pout. It is a perfectly suitable solution," he said casually.

"You slashed up my clothes! You cannot expect me to ride like this! It is indecent!"

"I can and I do. When you have calmed down, I will show you how to mount up." He turned away and checked the girth and stirrup straps. "Come here so we can adjust the length." She didn't move. "Hannah! We don't have all day. This will only be a short ride. It can take some getting used to. I couldn't walk for a week when I first started over at Yellow Creek. Riding for amusement does not have the same intensity as farm work. Now put your hands here so I can measure the length of the straps."

She shook her head bewildered. No inappropriate comments about her split skirt, or amusing quips about her trembling knees, just pragmatic instructions about where to stand, how to position her boot in the stirrup; sitting in the saddle; holding the reigns. Her skirt was forgotten as she focused on the horse, the reigns, the saddle, and transferring her weight down into the stirrups. It felt like the dance floor again, moving in time with the rhythm of the steps. She blinked hard as the back of her eyes started to sting. She realised then, as they rode slowly out towards the boundary, that she wanted to do this. She really did. To dance. To keep time. To work *on* this and *in* this together. And yet, she reminded herself, it could never be.

True to his word, it was a short lesson. Soon they were back in the yard, and he handed the reigns over to Toms while Sebastian helped her discreetly dismount. She stood and watched them ride out again almost straight away, talking together about the next undertaking. Peggy came up and stood by her side. "What is it, Miss? Is everything okay?"

"Yes Peggy. I guess so."

"I think you are brave to learn to ride so. Even George says it is unusual. He said he respects you for it, since you were not born to this. He reckons you and Mr Digby are matched in 'nerve and verve'."

"Hmm. Nerve and verve..." What she noticed about that observation was it would have been more meaningful to have the admiration of Sebastian. She wished he would notice her nerve as courage and not just irritation. "Well, Peggy perhaps you can learn riding too. I will ask Mr Digby if George can give you lessons."

"Oh Ma'am. Do you think so?"

"We are colonial girls now. I think George is right... we need all the *nerve and verve* we can muster. I am learning more than I ever thought possible. Now, I believe today we were going to tackle the cookhouse and the lay of the laundry to see if we could make it a bit friendlier. And I have some hemming to do on my riding habit. It has had some adjustments made to it."

The next morning Hannah woke stiff and sore. But she refused to give Sebastian any inkling that she was not up for the task. The lesson that morning was how to saddle the horse, and again they went out, this time further along the track. The following day, on an open stretch they broke into a light canter. And to Hannah's delight it wasn't terrifying. He gave her things to work on while he was away at Yellow Creek Station and promised that on his next home-days there would be longer riding excursions.

30.

They rode the horses even further out along the boundary line. Hannah's confidence was growing but she firmly refused to be drawn into any sort of competitive race to prove her proficiency. On the way home, Sebastian diverted the horses down along the line of the creek. They dismounted on a low gravel bar that was used as a crossing and let the horses drink. Under the cover of the trees Sebastian removed his rifle from its holster that hung by his saddle. He handed Hannah the reigns and walked a short distance away to make a shot. When he returned, he was dragging a wallaby behind him. Taking a rope from his saddle, he strung it up over a branch; and then using his knife, he bled it out. "I have done the shooting and fetching. The pantry is now restocked," he said. Finally, he wrapped it in a sheet stained with blood and slung it over the back of his horse, strapping it behind the saddle. He looked at her as he washed his knife and hands in the creek and then took a drink from his canvas canteen. "You are shocked that it is not only George who has been supplying meat for our table. Easier than shopping at the markets."

Hannah shook her head. "I doubt that you ever went to the markets, so I think that claim has little basis for comparison. I hardly know who you are anymore, Sebastian: you are so changed."

He shrugged. "We are all changed. Although, as I remember, both you and Aunt Biddy were relentless in advising that I amend my habits and demeanour. Well – here I am. Changed."

She swallowed and turned away. She was changed too.

He closed his eyes for a moment, but the frustration that simmered around him constantly refused to settle; now it flared up, ready to boil over. "Hannah, have you not yet forgiven me? Is it really so hopeless?"

"What do you mean?"

"I mean that I believed that if I gave you time you would see my sincerity. Even Mr Goon-ley once earnestly advised that I needed to take more time to aim my shot. It was probably the only sensible thing I could ever concede crossed his lips. I have been determined not to be impatient, but you try even the patience of a snail."

That forlorn familiar shadow passed across his eyes, and she reached out to take his hand. Energy surged through her at the touch, and she recoiled with a gasp and turned away, confused and flustered.

"What else do I need to do to show you I am genuine, Hannah? Surely you can see I will only be yours! I will never attempt another stunt like that night at the pub. I am so sorry." He stared at her back willing her to see sense. Why in this matter, when it mattered above all other matters, would she insist on being stupid? So very un-sensible. "All I wanted was to try and shake some semblance of jealousy from you."

"Well, you did. You really did," she murmured to herself in a moment of revelation. That was it exactly. She shook her head almost in despair.

"Does the list get longer?"

She turned to face him. "I told you the list does not exist, but if it had, I thought you realised that it was verified long ago."

"It was? Then why do you still hold out on me? Why are you so insistent on punishing me?"

"I hold out for just one thing. You know I do."

"I do?"

"I told you I want love. I meant a love that is reciprocated. Love that is not returned is just called obsession. I tire of my obsession with you, Sebastian!"

He studied her face and was shocked by what he saw there. "Are you mad?"

"So, madness is added to my list of crimes?"

"Surely you know I love you! How can you not?"

"You only say that I drive you crazy, and I exasperate you, and I shirk my responsibilities. Those things are not love or lovely. They are irritating and irresponsible, and it is humiliating to be constantly accused of being the cause."

"Hannah, what do I have to do? Yes, it drives me crazy to see you with another. If you talk about obsession, I am even more so! I take you visiting because I want the whole world... even the smallness of this new world... to know you are here. I allocate you the appropriate levels of regard and respect, even though you insist on being shuffled out the back like some shameful maid. I would not have it your way. Not once! You have always been my equal. And I have only ever treated you as such. You are the mistress of my home, partner in our livelihood and yet you insist on this remote formality. Please drop this nonsense and marry me!"

"Why would you marry someone who is a thorn in your side? That is pointless in this uncertain world of adversity!"

"But that is exactly my point! The only thing I am certain about in this place is you. Why else would I ask your opinion on things I am uncertain about?"

"The ballast? Again? Really Sebastian, why do I only function as sensible logic, a stabilizer, or a counterweight? That is not my idea of love. What about making life more tolerable in the hard and insufferable places? What about tenderness, and gentle care, or the ease of comfort? I wonder why I don't offer these benefits for you."

He burst out laughing and stood by his horse shaking his head.

"See, Mr Digby, you are not changed at all. You still cannot take anything seriously!"

"Can you not see we want the same thing? How many times have I ached to be tender… and yet you push me away with your sense of proper? You may never want for my attentions again. Wear my ring and I will take that as permission to be gentle and attentive and affectionate at every turn."

She leaned against her horse smelling the oiled leather and the horse sweat, and slowly lifted her gaze to meet his, perplexed by his declaration. Was it really true? Had she been blinkered to the obvious because it was not cloaked in the language, or even the ritual, she expected? She took a deep breath, and the whiff of this earthy reality settled over her like the comfort she had been seeking, and she realised it had been there all along. "Very well, Mr Digby. If you are serious… yes, I will marry you."

"If I am serious? I'm as serious as an undertaker. This is a very serious matter."

"Once again, you are not being convincing, Mr Digby."

"It would be worth marrying just for the relief of never having to hear you call me Mr Digby again," he said with a grin. He came around by her side, and drew her away from the horse, lifted her up and spun her around in a twirl, and took a few steps of a dance. "You doubt if I am serious? I seriously consider it done!" He reached into the pocket lining of his jacket and pulled out a dark leather pouch. He opened it and took out a familiar lace kerchief; he gently opened the folds on the palm of his hand and held up his mother's ring. "When my mother gave this to me, she said it represented an 'unbroken circle'. It belongs on your hand, Hannah. You are the piece needed for this circle to be whole. Allow me to offer this to you as my bride, as you once so aptly stipulated?"

"You brought the ring with you? Is that just a little presumptuous?" she said with a smile.

"I have carried it with me since you returned it. I did not want to miss my moment. Will you wear it now? Please!"

She nodded. He slipped it on her finger and their hands intermeshed. She stared at his fingers intertwined in hers wearing his ring, roughened by work; and felt the same intertwining of their hearts, roughened by life. She shyly allowed herself to be enveloped tenderly in his arms as he kissed her forehead, swaying again in the rhythm of a slow waltz, feeling him close.

"Finally," he sighed as he tucked a stray strand of hair behind her ear, "My glamorous little maid-and-cook. Finally."

Epilogue

Hannah took the coins from her purse and laid them on the counter. Just then she heard the customer behind her gasp and swear under his breath. Hannah made every effort to ignore his rudeness and refused to look at him. She stoically returned her change to her purse and picked up her meagre parcels. She turned away and made for the door. How dare people be so ignorant? They did not know what they had gone through or the progress they had made. So much had happened: the rebuilding; establishing their stock; seeing their hard work ebb away in the agony of drought; and then the joy that drought-breaking rain brought. Fallowhytes was coming alive again. These shopping excursions, even though they may appear unimpressive, were greatly anticipated.

She turned and walked up the dusty street. She heard his step behind her, and she quickened her pace. "Ma'am? Ma'am!" Hannah refused to turn but briefly glanced down the street and crossed over. He followed her, his long stride soon caught up with her and he fell in step. "Ma'am? I need to ask. In the shop back there, I saw your ring. It is quite unique, and I wondered where you got it."

"Sir! The accusation is quite unnecessary. It was given to me by my husband. I wear it as a declaration of his love and my commitment to him."

"Oh, Ma'am my apologies for seeming intrusive. But it is stunning, and it reminded me of a ring that belonged to a dear friend of mine."

Hannah stopped. "Sir I will not sell it. It belonged to my husband's mother. I could not possibly part with it."

"Oh, I do not expect you to part with something so beautiful. I really just wanted to know it's story... just perchance that a similar ring may hold a similar story."

"To be honest I don't know its story. Sebastian said it belonged to his mother, and he always anticipated giving it to his bride. That is really all I know."

"Sebastian?"

"Yes... my husband." She thought he was being very nosey, and she didn't think that his fabricated interest in a piece of jewellery warranted the questions he was asking. "Sir I feel that you are being far too..."

"Sebastian Digby?"

That shocked her. "Sir! How would you know that?" And then she felt foolish that he had extracted his name from her. She turned to go, and firmly set out to meet the others back at the hotel as they agreed.

He followed her quickly. "I know his uncle: Mr Edward Whitmore."

That declaration stopped her in her tracks. "Uncle Eddie? How...? I don't understand. Are you investigating us?"

"He is... a close family... friend."

"Sir, it evidently cannot be too close an association, or you would know that he has passed on."

"Eddie? Gone? Oh." He frowned and swallowed hard.

Something in his eyes elicited compassion in Hannah's heart. "Oh, I'm sorry Sir. I forget the divide of oceans from the Mother of the Empire. Did you know his wife?"

"Biddy? Oh, my goodness yes. *Did*? Tell me she is alive and well."

"Aunt Biddy is very much alive."

He relaxed and smiled in a disarming way. "Ahh Biddy. We've had some laughs."

Laughs? That didn't seem very appropriate. She checked herself. "Sir. You must understand this is very bizarre. I think it would be best if you come with me so that you can verify your tale." She walked a few steps and then stopped dead. "Yet you haven't told me *your* name," she accused. "Are you Mr Jack White?" She searched his face for a likeness, but the greying beard and the low-slung hat really didn't seem to allow it to be possible. But the creases around his blue eyes did seem familiar. "Oh, my goodness. You are. You are him! You are Mr White!"

"I am?" He looked at her and smiled mischievously. "Yes, I believe you are correct. I am Jack White."

She shuffled him to the side of the walkway. "Well you can't see Aunt Biddy," she said lowering her voice.

"Why not?" he whispered in return. His eyes creased deeper in amusement as he mirrored her low tone.

"She doesn't know!" she whispered forcefully.

"What Biddy doesn't know is hardly worth knowing. I must see her! Why are we whispering?"

"Sebastian has not told her about the letter. She doesn't know! No, you cannot see her."

"Letter?" His voice returned to normal. "Well... I think Biddy is probably the best person to clarify that. If I know her at all, I would bet that she knows at least some of what she is not intended to know."

Hannah started to breathe heavily. "Oh Sir… I don't feel well. I really don't know what to…"

"Hannah? Is this man bothering you?" Sebastian strode to her side and quickly supported her arm.

She leant on it hard. "Sebastian… this is Mr…"

He turned and his eyes went wide. "Jonathon! Is that you? What are you doing here Uncle?" And he flung his arms around him in a fierce embrace.

"Mr… Mr Jack White," she finished lamely. Then she took another deep breath and passed out.

Sebastian carried her to the hotel and laid her on a lounge and fanned her face with a paper. "Someone, fetch a glass of water!" he ordered, as her eyes came back into focus.

"Oh… I don't feel well," she whimpered.

"Here… take a drink. Peggy! Go and fetch Aunt Biddy. Now!"

Hannah held up her hand. "He saw the ring. He followed me. He is not your Uncle… he is Jack White. Jack White of the letter. He is…" She started gasping again and couldn't continue.

Aunt Biddy came and with pursed lips began to wipe Hannah's pale face. She pulled out a fan started waving it over her vigorously. "Do you believe me now child? If you can't go shopping without passing out, surely that is evidence enough that you are in the family way. If you think otherwise, I am losing my…" She glanced around at the gathered faces and stood up straight. "Oh."

Jonathon stood there grinning. Biddy matched his gaze, wordless.

Sebastian crouched down beside Hannah with a confused frown, staring at her with an open mouth. "Are you…?"

Peggy offered to fetch everyone tea. Hannah started breathing heavily again. Sebastian's legs folded underneath him and he ended up sitting on the floor beside Hannah lying on the chaise. "Family?" he said weakly, with a silly grin on his face.

Eventually, Aunt Biddy smoothed her skirt slowly and quietly turned to Peggy before she sat down. "I think tea is an excellent idea."

When they poured their cups, everyone started talking at once.

"So, you think you are?" Sebastian asked again.

"I believe so… but I wanted to be sure." Hannah sat up and took the teacup offered to her. "It has been so long, I hardly dared hope…"

Aunt Biddy took up her cup and saucer. "Jonathon? Where on earth did you come from? We heard you were in the Americas."

"Been here for years. Yes, I go by Jack White: Jonathon – Jack. Whitmore – White. Seemed reasonable and less ostentatious for the colonial mind. I bumped into the oldest Digby a few years back… Roderick. We had not met previously, but he was pretty free with his talk. I never told him who I was. Heard he left."

"Roderick had the wrong idea about you, which is why we are here. He was the genius behind getting us exiled," said Sebastian pulling his attention back to the group.

"He was?" said Aunt Biddy with a frown. "I thought this was your father's initiative."

"From the same viper's nest. He's like his old man," said Jack. "Australia is known for its snakes. But we usually don't have to import them. Still, one day you may thank him."

"Huh. I'm thinking more and more, it is not bad that we are out from under all that," said Sebastian.

"Well, it seems you have done well with him, Biddy. He's different from the other Digby's. Perhaps he is his mother's son after all."

Biddy took a sip of tea, and murmured under her breath, "Or his father's."

Sebastian licked his lips like he wanted them to work properly. "Roderick told Father that you and my mother… were…" Hannah squeezed his hand hard. Sebastian paused, looked at her hand clutching his with white knuckles and then stared at his uncle. Their eyes connected… and he considered the possibility of what others had pieced together. Jack looked confused and Aunt Biddy's cup rattled ungainly in her saucer.

Eventually, Aunt Biddy took another sip of tea. "She never told you, did she?"

Jack shook his head. "Who? Told me what?"

"Beth. That Sebastian is not Tyndale's son. He is yours."

"You knew?" said Sebastian and Hannah together.

Aunt Biddy flashed them a look. "Beth never told anyone and made me promise on her deathbed that I would never tell. I never have… until now. How could *you* possibly know this?"

Sebastian took the confession by the throat. "Roderick guessed it. He said he had met a Jack White who looked too similar for it to be coincidence." He blinked hard and swallowed. "I don't believe it! I am truly a Whitmore," he said, the relief of his exoneration was heady.

"Pish-posh and twaddle, Sebastian. You have been a Whitmore for a long time. The name is the least of it."

"Well, that furtive little conjecture was Roderick's leverage to go home. We found his drafted letter in the box of records on the ship, addressed to Father."

"Well, he leveraged his way into Whytehaven Hall, that is for certain," said Aunt Biddy with a sprinkling of resentment she had never aired in relation to her eviction before.

"He's at Whytehaven? But he's not next in line," said Jack.

"Well no. But no one knew where you were. They declared you officially missing… deceased. We have no heir, so it goes from Whitmore to Digby's."

Jack stared at Biddy and the creases around his weathered eyes deepened. "Well, what do you know? Technically Whytehaven was mine as next in line after Eddie… and then it would go to the kid as my son – legitimate or otherwise. You knew all along… and yet you said nothing. You could have stayed."

"Beth asked me not to speak of it. I had no choice."

"So, you came. And here you are… forging your own mark, ruling this new realm with that same Bridget poise. Eddie would be proud of you Biddy." In that moment, their eyes locked, and the room faded out of focus.

Hannah felt like she was walking through a maze. "Did you give this ring to Sebastian's mother? Is that why you recognised it?"

He drew his attention back to the others. "I did. I found it in a wonderful Persian Bazaar. I've never seen another like it. After I gave it to Beth, I tried to convince her to leave with me. She almost agreed but then she found out she was pregnant. She said that was why she needed to stay; she felt she was obligated to give her baby the opportunities that a life abroad could never offer. Beth told me the baby was Tyndale's, and it was her chance for redemption. She believed that Digby would respond to this baby since they didn't have a child together, and the boys from his first marriage were much older. I didn't have her faith... but of course she wouldn't leave. After she died, I left for America. Wandered from there to Africa, ended up in Cape Town... and it just seemed a natural course to check out Australia as well."

"And you never guessed... that I was not a Digby?"

"I can see it now. But back then you were the kid that kept us apart. Still, we had good times at Whytehaven. The invitations from Biddy always came when you were home from the Academy. I've got to confess you didn't seem cut from Digby cloth. Beth's insistence on keeping you at Whytehave rather than with Digby's lot seemed the difference. But then, what is the making of schoolmasters, or the influence of Eddie and Biddy, and what was your mother? Sometimes it seemed possible, and other times... just mere fancy."

Aunt Biddy closed her eyes and inhaled some more tea. "Well, she told me, so fancy is off the table."

Jack said nothing for a while. "Huh. After all these years of wanderlust... I find out I am a father... and becoming a grandfather is thrown into the mix for good measure. All in one day! It doesn't get bigger than that. Beth would have enjoyed the momentous nature of this moment. Oh, she would!" And he burst out laughing.

Aunt Biddy smiled. "Oh yes, that is true. That is certainly true. She always had such unwavering faith for..."

"... unbroken circles," said Sebastian and Hannah together.

Coming soon from Olwyn Harris: Pioneers of Grace Series

Book 3 - Journey of Grace

Tibby had grand dreams that were very different from the squalor of the textile mill tenements where she grew up. She plotted her escape by taking sponsored passage to the Colony as a bride, but everything on this journey was harder than even she could imagine. Dumped like garbage at the gate of Zachary Logan's place, will it be possible for Tabitha to sew a new life together in this barren wasteland of Australia?

Book 4 - Mask of Grace

Late one night, Martha finds herself at a wayside inn, running from the expectations of her family. To stay in hiding, she works as a scullery maid alongside Simmons, who doesn't just cook, but is a culinary artist. Intrigued by each other's secrets, will they be able to drop their pretence long enough to find their true passions?

Book 5 – Crucible of Grace

Ruth has had more than her fair share of tragedy. When her widowed mother-in-law wants to return to the farming region where her family once thrived, Ruth works as a laundry maid to support them. Can Ruth survive the fire of heartache and prejudice to find a new shape for her life, which might even include the station owner?

Book 6 – Sculpture of Grace

Rachel loves her country life. She loves her art of forging iron and her growing friendship with the station's newest blacksmith. Leah, her older sister, on the other hand, does not like anything country. But, as fate would have it, Rachel is offered a proposal which means she would have to leave the valley she loves, while Leah is sidelined and mourns her dreams of more. Can the sisters find a way to reconcile their destinies and forge a different story where they both see their dreams come true?

#1 The Beachside Cottage

In this offering from Olwyn Harris, we meet the heartbroken and downtrodden Eliza-Beth Perkins. Eliza-Beth is facing the dire consequences of her choices and the possibility of life in the poorhouse. Then she, literally, runs into Jensen Harker. Jensen is facing his own heartbreak at the death of his wife and wants nothing more than to be left alone. But something in Eliza-Beth stirs him to make a rash proposal, thus rescuing her from her predicament. As we follow their journey together, will we see them find the healing they both desperately need?

#2 Petrea Downs

In the 2nd book in this series, we meet Meg. Meg's life has been turned upside-down, with her husband gone, trying to run Petrea Downs by herself, and disaster after disaster at every turn. Thankfully, her neighbour Everett Grossman is always there to help. The final blow comes when a cattle duffer tries to steal her only source of income, gets shot, and has to be nursed back to health in her living room. But, is Ben Harker really the villain he seems? And is Everett really the hero he makes himself out to be?

#3 The Writer's Retreat

The third book in the Homes of Healing trilogy introduces us to Tess, a romance writer, who prides herself on letting her characters tell their own story. When she arrives at Rocky Creek B&B, the run-down stone cottage looks like the perfect place for her to retreat to, not only to write her book, but to escape her past. Join her as she discovers her characters and explores their stories, and finds that God Is intent on becoming part of her own story at the same time. As her relationship with the local publican challenges her to stop running, she realises that real life and real love can be messy and complicated. Can she honestly confront the ugly aspects in her own story, so that God can bring them both to a place of healing?

#1 Sapphires of Hope

"There is no way," she thought, "that I am going to use this!" She had desperately searched their cupboards for something, anything that would come close to what she needed for her catering project. She found only this old dilapidated breadbasket that looked like the sort of junk that comes from one of those tacky jumble-sale stalls..."

Andi and Jo are best friends... they do pretty much everything together. So, when Andi has a catering assignment due, and only a tacky old basket to use, Jo helps her pull off the faded decorations, revealing a time-capsule of historical information, and in order to understand what it means, Andi and Jo ask their elderly neighbour to take them to visit the farm where the basket came from. They find themselves dumped back in history at the time of Federation, embroiled in circumstances that nearly cost Andi her life and threatens the livelihood of the people living there. How can they ever hope to keep going when things are spinning out of control?

#2 Rubies of Ambition

In the 2nd book in the Gem of Australia series, we again travel with Andi and Jo back in time. On this adventure, they meet the very beautiful and ambitious actress, Lillian Browning, who is on the run from the federal police. Andi and Jo accompany her back to her hometown, where they find she is not well received. Will Lillian find a balance between the past that calls her and the ambitions that drive her?

#3 Emerald Dreams

In the third installment of the *Gems of Australia* series, Olwyn Harris brings Australian history to life as she takes us on a journey back to the early days of convict settlement in Australia. Here we, once again, find Andi and Jo learning about Australia's true history, and finding strength in God to help others.

#1: A Spacious Place

In this first instalment of the Guthrie's Lot series, set in the late 1800s, we meet Irvin Guthrie, a practical, no-nonsense man with a sick wife and a small child to care for. When his wife's doctor suggests they move to a warmer climate, he spends everything he has on a property that ends up not being what he expected.

Joanna Grenham has dreams of being a schoolteacher. When an opportunity presents itself, she jumps at the chance, only to find herself given no choice but to care for Irvin's sick wife and child.

Will Irvin and Joanna make the most of their circumstances, or will they forever find life as hard and unyielding as the ground in A Spacious Place.

#2: A Level Path

In the second instalment of the Guthrie's Lot series, it is now the late 1960s. Here we meet Irvin's granddaughter Iris. Iris hungers for excitement and adventure, and she won't find that in Gumleigh, or with the ever-predictable Dave. The last thing she expected was for Dave to follow her across the world to England as she tries to find direction and meaning.

Will Iris finally see through the charismatic, but ultimately selfish, Stan, or will Dave leave England alone and leave Iris to find her own way to A Level Path?

#3: The Crying Tree

In this final episode of the Guthrie's Lot series, the year is now 2010. We meet Mac, who has always been an achiever – a do-er, just like her father. After the death of her mother, she finds that she needs to get away, so she buys a little run-down stone cottage in the middle of nowhere to transform into a creative studio. She is taken by the feel of the place - especially the twisted weeping willow tree behind the house, even though it doesn't fit into her plans anywhere.

Dan spent years growing up on the old Guthrie place, so when the new owner arrives, he is not convinced that he wants to work for this headstrong woman, who is obviously used to getting what she wants, but he feels that it is something he has to do – and only God knows why.

Can Dan and Mac work together to make her dreams into a reality? Will she transform the old Guthrie place, and her life, into something unique and beautiful? And what will become of Thy Crying Tree.

Matt's Boys of Wattle Creek

When Matthew Lawson's three sons were born, he wrote each of them a letter outlining his hopes and prayers for their futures. When he decided to give up his city job and move to the little town of Wattle Creek, he could never have imagined the effect it would have on his young family. As Matt's boys grow to maturity and find their places in their community, will his dreams and prayers come to fulfilment? Will his boys develop their own faith in the eternal God? And will they each find the kind of love that Matt holds for his beautiful Josie?

Maggie & Minotaur

"For Maggie, the mythical Minotaur represented Romance – half man, half beast. The Minotaur was a monster created from centuries of classical Greek mythology and no normal man could withstand its strength...... Sooner or later she would accept that Theseus, the hero, did not exist. She knew that she would have to battle through the maze of reality and confront it herself...." Maggie Wick was shipped off to the city and high society life at the age of 12, where she would learn the ways of the rich and marry into a family of influence. What could have caused her sudden return to Henderson's Gap? Can she really settle back into life on the station, with all its diversity and challenges? Will she find fulfilment in her role as provisional schoolteacher? Will she ever figure out the "Captain", the mysterious, intimidating, station manager? When war comes to her little haven and Maggie's world comes crashing down, taking her loved ones and the captain with it, Maggie needs to find a way to survive. Will her faith be enough to protect her, and what of the Captain? Could he really be the Theseus who would do battle with her Minotaur?

The Bush Olympics

The Bush Olympics, written by Olwyn Harris and beautifully illustrated by Shelly Askew, shows us that we don't have to be good at everything to be part of a team. Even sleepy Koala is good at something, and if everyone plays their part, we can all be successful together.